ALDO

MEN OF THE FALLS BOOK 1

NEW YORK TIMES AND *USA TODAY* BESTSELLING AUTHOR

MELANIE MORELAND

ALDO - Book 1 Men Of The Falls
by Melanie Moreland

Paperback 978-1-99-080373-4

MORELAND
BOOKS INC.

Edited by Lisa Hollett of Silently Correcting Your Grammar
Proofreading by Sisters Get Lit.erary Services
Cover design by Feed Your Dreams Designs

Readers with concerns about content or subjects depicted can check out the content advisory on my website: https://melaniemoreland.com/extras/fan-suggestions/content-advisory/

Aldo Ricci

Right hand to Roman Costas.

Enforcer. Loyal.

Alone. Happy to stay that way.

Until she walks into his life.

Violet Nelson

Unexpected. Alluring. Off-limits.

But he can't stay away.

The last thing he expected from her was the one thing he'd never sought.

Redemption.

DEDICATION

For the girl who asked so nicely

I couldn't say no.

Thank you.

Beth – this is for you.

CHAPTER 1
ALDO

I sat down at the desk in the office I shared with Roman Costas—my boss. It was one of many offices in the large building that housed a first-class hotel and casino in Niagara Falls. We called this one the war room. The glass wall on the one end gave us an overview of the casino below. We used it a lot. We strategized. Budgeted. Discussed.

I mostly used another office close to the casino, Roman only joining me there on occasion. I conducted interviews, met with employees, and worked there when I needed some space. Roman had his own personal office on the top floor of the hotel. It was accessed by a private elevator and was attached to a suite he spent many nights in. There was a connected suite used exclusively by his nonna. No one and nothing were allowed on that part of the floor unless given permission by Roman himself. Very few of us had access.

Then there was the "office" in the basement. It was one you didn't want to be invited to. Chances were, if you were, you wouldn't walk out. Or if you did, you had learned a very valuable and painful lesson.

Never to cross Roman Costas.

I poured a cup of coffee, inhaling the aroma of the rich liquid. I let my mind wander, thinking of the first time I had met Roman. We'd both been eight. My mother had gone to work for the Costas family. Roman's mother was a pretty lady and a kind employer. My father worked for their father as a driver. I only ever spied Mr. Costas on occasion, and when I did, I stayed out of the way. We lived in a small house on the other side of their large estate north of Toronto. Roman and I became good friends, bonding over trucks. His brother Luca joined us often, the three of us playing together. Life was normal. As normal as I knew it.

And then, three years later, Mrs. Costas died. Everything changed. Their already distant father became more withdrawn and cold.

Playing was not allowed for the brothers. Or laughter. Martial arts, shooting lessons, intense study took center stage. A sense of darkness hovered over the house. As the boys grew older, Mr. Costas pitted the brothers against each other, rewarding the victor, punishing the loser. He “taught” them lessons no kids should learn. They witnessed violence continuously. Roman loathed it. Luca despised it. Both endured.

Nonna came to live with them not long after their mother died. She was the one thing in their life that prevented them from becoming like their father. She kept them together, constantly reminding them of their bond as brothers. As family. Without her, I was certain the brothers would have become replicas of their father. But she kept the spirit of their gentler mother alive within them. When Mr. Costas was away, which was often, the house was different, the boys freer. But as soon as he stepped through the doorway, the silence would descend. They hid huge pieces of themselves away from him, knowing he would destroy those parts. Nonna fed those and kept the light alive, all while seemingly bowing to Mr. Costas’s demands.

As the years went by, Roman and I remained tight. I was allowed to be around because of my father, but I wasn’t considered one of them. At least, not to their father. To Roman and, even to some extent, Luca, I was a brother and treated as such. Nonna V accepted me and loved me as one of her own. When my own mother died of cancer when I was thirteen, she became the soft spot for me I was missing. When I was eighteen, my father had a heart attack—Roman, Luca, and Nonna V became my only family.

And thanks to the unexpected growth spurt I had when I was sixteen, I became Roman's right hand and undeclared security. At six foot five, I wasn't messed with. Thanks to my love of using exercise to work out my frustrations, I was broad, strong, and, according to Roman, serious.

I liked to tell him my intensity came from copying him. It was rare to see a smile on his face, unless we were in private. For a few years, I never saw one.

Once his father died, that changed.

Everything changed.

The door opening made me look up. Roman strode in, looking tired and sporting a bruise to his cheekbone. He poured himself a cup of coffee and sat down at his desk with a long sigh.

"Fuck me, is today over?" he muttered.

I chuckled, glancing at my watch. "It's nine a.m., Roman."

"Great."

"You been going a few rounds with your trainer?" I indicated the bruise on his face.

"Luca."

I was surprised. The brothers rarely fought.

He leaned back in his chair, shutting his eyes. "I deserved it."

"Now there's a story I have to hear."

He sat up, picking up his coffee and taking a drink. "We had dinner last night with some business associates."

"This business or that business?"

"Both," Roman replied. "They're legit, but they have ties to the syndicate as well. They're part of my generation."

Roman and Luca had changed a lot of things since their father died, including who they dealt with.

"So Mason asked a favor. His sister, Justine, is coming to town for a visit. Surprisingly, she has never been to Toronto. He's worried about her and wants me to keep an eye on her. Take her out and show her Toronto."

"You said no, and Luca punched you on his behalf?"

"I said no and volunteered Luca."

I chuckled. I understood the punch now. Luca hated blind dates—even more so than Roman. Neither man liked relationships of any sort.

"I said I was here too much, and Luca already lived in Toronto and it made more sense. And I might have made all the arrangements without consulting Luca.

When he arrived, it was all set." Roman grinned. "He showed his displeasure afterward. I am, apparently, footing the bill for him playing tourist guide."

We both laughed. Roman ran his hand through his chestnut-colored hair, and his green eyes were amused. "It was worth it. He couldn't say shit while Mason was sitting at the table. I knew he wasn't pleased, although he accepted it graciously in front of Mason. Once we were in my suite, however…"

"He drilled you."

"Basically. But he is still taking her out. Better him than me. The last thing I need is a syndicate princess around, wanting to be taken places. The list Mason had was long and boring as hell. Spare me."

"How old is she?"

"Late twenties, which seems a bit old for needing an escort, but Mason is incredibly protective of her, which, frankly, bodes badly for Luca."

"Knowing Luca, it's gonna cost you."

"It'll be worth it not to have to dance to her tune. Whatever it is. She sent him a text last night with more of her demands. Luca already despises her. He got the feeling she felt the same way. She called him her jailer. He called her a spoiled princess." Roman flashed his teeth. "Maybe they'll bond over it."

I laughed with him again. It was nice to see him in a good mood for a change.

"Anyway, it was a long meeting, and then Nonna wanted me to have breakfast with her."

"How is she?"

He smiled fondly. "A tyrant as usual. She was getting ready to go inspect the grapes with the foreman. In other words, tell him what to do."

I chuckled. Nonna V was a powerhouse. She had more energy in her seventies than I had on my best day. Roman had a large winery and house in the Niagara region. She lived with him and ran the estate. He went back and forth between the house and his suite here, always busy. But he adored her and refused to let her live on her own. She was equally fierce in her love for her daughter's youngest child. He looked like his mother and always said that was the reason his father disliked him so much. Looking at Roman had been too painful.

"She wants you to come to lunch on Sunday. Says she hasn't seen you in forever."

"Two weeks, you mean."

He shrugged. "You argue semantics with her."

I adored Nonna V as well, and I never turned down a lunch invitation.

"I'll be there."

"Anything concerning here?"

"No. Everything is smooth. I have some final applicants for the waitress jobs to look over. We hired the new dealers and the front of house for the hotel. You need to be there tomorrow for the meet-and-greet."

Roman and I had a policy that we met every new employee. Shook their hand. Let them see who they were working for. Roman owned everything. I was his right hand. We worked as a team, and one of us was usually on hand if needed. If not, we were never far away and always reachable. We had a handpicked group of managers, assistants, security, and staff. Each manager was responsible for their division. Hard work and loyalty were rewarded. Mediocre effort was not acceptable. Each and every problem was solved immediately. The Maple was the best of the best. Roman accepted nothing less. His second casino in Toronto, Maple II, was the same.

He finished his coffee. "I'll let you get on, then. I have some money to move and some contracts to go over. I'll grab some sleep and do the late shift."

I nodded and he left, shutting the door behind him. I wondered if he would sleep. He got only a few hours at a time, always too restless and on edge to relax. As his friend, I worried about him, but he refused to listen or alter his ways.

I shook my head, knowing worrying about it would do nothing. Roman was Roman, and he would never change.

Then I chuckled. I was almost as bad as he was. This place was my life, and I didn't see that changing anytime soon.

If ever.

CHAPTER 2
ALDO

I returned to my other office and perused the résumé of the people I would be interviewing today. I vetted every person we hired. I handled the final interviews. Always. Once I approved them, I washed my hands of them and turned them over to their respective managers. But I always had the last say before that. I had a knack for knowing if the person was the right fit.

I had never been wrong.

I flipped through the pages, stopping on one résumé. Each one had a photo. It was part of our process. We never discriminated on someone's looks or ethnicity, but I ran the photos of the candidates through special software we had. Given Roman's ties to the criminal world, we could never be too careful.

Something about the woman in the photo gave me pause. She was lovely. Her dark brown hair was short, hanging around her ears and showing off a long, elegant neck. She had a wide smile, and her hazel eyes were mischievous. There was something appealing about her. I shook my head and dismissed that thought. I must need to get laid. It had been a while.

One thing Luca, Roman, and I all agreed on was our views on relationships. None of us was interested in one—much to Nonna V's disappointment. Luca was a serial dater, Roman never dated, only having the occasional one-night stand, and I did even less. Most women I met were for the evening sort of relationship. A hotel room might be involved or, occasionally, not. Given the world we knew and dwelled in, it was better for all of us to remain unencumbered.

My phone rang, and I shut the file, putting it into order and forgetting the woman. I answered the phone and told my assistant to send in the first applicant.

The next few hours went past quickly. Most of those I interviewed were fine. Two were definite strikes. Their answers were so textbook, I knew they would be lousy employees once they came on board.

And then she arrived.

The hazel-eyed, lovely woman from the file. Violet Nelson.

She walked in, and it felt as if all the air had been sucked out of the room. Something flexed in my chest as she came closer, and I stood to greet her.

She was tall. Curvy. Heavy breasts, legs that went on for miles. And her smile?

Killer.

I was on autopilot as I shook her hand, introduced myself, and indicated for her to take a seat. She did so, crossing her sexy legs and showing me a glimpse of smooth skin before she gathered the folds of her skirt underneath her. She grinned, looking sheepish, but I had a feeling she didn't feel that way.

I chose to ignore it and the way my cock kicked up in my pants at the sight of that creamy-looking calf.

Obviously, it had been way too long for me if the flash of some skin did that.

But I would think about that later.

"So, Violet, I see you just moved here from Toronto. Why the change, if I may ask?"

"My boyfriend made the decision for me."

My eyebrows lifted of their own accord. She didn't look like the type who would let her boyfriend decide on something that big.

"He took a job here?"

"He took off with the contents of my apartment and bank account, along with my so-called best friend, Marie. I heard a couple women talking about the hotel and the jobs here. I had nothing left in Toronto, so I took a chance and came here."

I had no idea how to respond. What I did say shocked me. "You want me to find him and kill him?"

She threw back her head in laughter. "Oh, you're funny, big man. Thanks, but I'm good."

I nodded, offering a tight smile. I hadn't been joking.

"You checked off the casual dining restaurant. Why?"

"I think it's better suited to me. I'm not formal, and I wouldn't do well at the buffet. I think the people at the deli-style restaurant would be good to handle. They aren't looking to stay a long time, they'll want their food, be in and out, so the turnover would be good. And the more I serve, the better the tips."

I liked her honesty.

"I see you've had experience."

"Put myself through high school and bought my first car with waitressing. I was working as a receptionist, but that job vanished after Covid. I've been with a temp agency. I can provide references."

I had already checked them out, and she had glowing reports. Punctual, honest, hardworking, were some of the words to describe her.

"And nights and evenings are okay for you?"

"Yes."

I scanned her file, not recognizing the street address. "Where are you living now?"

"Kelly's Kourt until I find something permanent."

I winced. That was a rougher part of the city and a run-down motel where you could rent by the hour, day, or week. I met her eyes, but hers held no apology or pity for herself.

"It's only temporary," she insisted. "Once I work a bit, I can have first and last."

She was proud. I detected a stubborn streak. And I had the feeling she suffered no fools, so she wouldn't take any shit from the customers. I thought she would do well in our formal dining room. It was hard to get into, and the waiting list was long. I could see her in the uniform. All the staff wore the same thing. A black tux. On the men, it looked classy, and on the women, sexy. On her, I imagined it would be art. Dead sexy art.

But she wanted casual. Perhaps she would change her mind.

I signed the last form in her file and handed it to her. "HR is on the right at the end of the hall. They'll take all your information. You'll report to Wanda, who will give you your uniform and schedule. You can start right away." I paused and wrote some information on another piece of paper. "Mayburn Apartments on Third. Clean, reasonable. Tell the manager I sent you. He'll waive first and last until you can afford it."

She blinked. Then blinked again. "Thank you, Mr. Ricci. I appreciate it."

I waved her off. "We take care of our employees here."

She stood and offered her hand. I shook it, wondering why her skin felt so right sliding along mine. Why her grip felt perfect within mine. I looked down, noticing how creamy and soft her skin looked compared to my darker, sun-kissed hue. It was night and day. Like we were.

Like we would remain. Two different orbits.

I didn't fuck employees, and she wasn't looking for what I could offer her.

She left and I sat down, shaking my head, then picking up the phone and calling the manager of Mayburn Apartments. Brian Ferris and his wife liked to gamble. They came every few weeks and enjoyed a day here, eating in the restaurant, never going over their allotted budget. I had gotten to know them, and he owed me a favor for something I had done for him. He was happy to accept my word on first and last and told me he had a studio open at the moment.

"Make sure she gets it," I said and hung up.

I had no idea why I had made the offer or the call.

I was simply being nice to someone who was down on their luck.

It had nothing to do with that killer smile.

Or those fucking dead sexy legs.

Nothing.

CHAPTER 3
VIOLET

HR was swift and efficient. Like everything else I had seen in this hotel, it was run like a well-oiled machine. I was escorted to meet Wanda, who was an older woman, cordial and well put-together. She gave me a tour, nodding in satisfaction as I asked for a menu to study.

"I'll bring it back my first shift."

"I like you," she said.

In the back, she indicated the shelves of uniforms. "You get two," she said. "Take your size. Once you've done your three-week probation, you get two more. You can buy additional, and they are replaced every couple of months. Mr. Costas insists the staff look smart."

I looked at the samples on the wall. I loved the slim black trousers and white shirt, the logo embroidered on the pocket. And the polka-dot skirt with a different short-sleeved shirt. It was cute and fun. The clothes had a fifties theme, and I loved it. There were two other options, but I chose those.

"You have good shoes?" she asked. "We get a discount at White's." She showed me her athletic shoes. "You get one pair after the probation too."

"I have some until then." I couldn't really afford shoes at the moment.

"And you're good for nights and weekends? Those are the hardest shifts to fill."

"I'll take as many as you can give."

"I can start training you tomorrow."

"Awesome." I glanced around. "Can you tell me a cheap place to park? Or should I take the bus?"

"Staff has a dedicated floor. Basement level two. You need a pass, and it's five dollars a day."

I grinned. "Let me guess. After probation?"

She laughed. "No, I can give you a temporary one. I just need your car details."

She wrote down the info and handed me a pass, giving me directions on how to get it.

"So, tomorrow. Six p.m. to two a.m. There is a meet-and-greet tomorrow afternoon in the ballroom. The owner meets every new employee."

The woman in HR had mentioned that already, so I was prepared. "That is a great concept. Very classy."

She nodded. "Everything at the Maple is classy. The event is at three, so it'll be a long day for you, but you can have your meal if you want."

"My meal?"

"You get a meal and a snack with every full shift. A snack with a half."

I was impressed. "I met Mr. Ricci earlier."

She nodded. "He is Mr. Costas's right hand. The senior manager of the whole place. You won't have much to do with them, but they do this after every set of hires. Meet the new staff."

"I'll be there."

She smiled. "Welcome to the Maple, Violet."

I left, clutching the bag with my uniforms. Outside, I slid on my sunglasses and walked to my car. I had parked a long way away since it was cheaper. I used my phone GPS and located the apartment building Mr. Ricci had instructed me to check out. It was a small structure—only four stories high, but the neighborhood was decent and the building was well-kept. Brian Ferris and his wife Fran showed me the studio apartment on the second floor. It was small but clean. One room with a tiny kitchen in the corner, a counter separating it from the rest of the living area. A compact bathroom was on the opposite side, along with the only closet.

"They left the sofa. We'll get rid of it unless you want it?" Fran asked. "It's pretty new and clean."

"That would be great."

"When can you move in?"

"Now." I only had two suitcases and two boxes. My jerk of an ex had sold or stolen everything else. And I never left a thing at the hotel. It was safer in the back of my car than in the room. I was certain someone was in there every day when I left to job search. And they weren't cleaning. It gave me the creeps, but it was all I could afford.

Brian looked surprised, but Fran nodded. "Where have you been staying?"

"Kelly's Kourt."

Fran grimaced. "You need help moving in?"

"No, I just have a few things."

She handed me the key. "Brian will bring the papers to you."

I closed my hand around the cold metal. "Thank you."

I carried up my suitcases and the boxes, setting them on the floor. I checked out the small kitchen. Everything had been cleaned, which I was grateful for. The bathroom was tiny, but it was fine. It wasn't forever. I walked a few blocks up and had a burger at a fast-food place, then stopped at the grocery store and bought some items. It would be a couple of weeks until I got a paycheck, so when I got back to the apartment, I sat on the surprisingly comfortable sofa and counted my money. That bastard Barry had figured out my passcode and emptied my modest savings account and cleared my apartment of anything valuable.

In hindsight, I should have known better. Barry was too charming, too good-looking. He was, as it turned out, also lazy, a liar, and a thief. We hadn't been dating long when his apartment was "flooded" and he asked to stay with me for a few days. A few days became a few weeks. Then he was gone. With my money, my stuff, and my backstabbing friend. I went to the building he had told me he lived in, only to find they had never heard of him.

I had been conned. I hoped Marie got dumped somewhere and left stranded.

Luckily, he never touched the two boxes in the bedroom closet or my clothes. Probably because he ran out of time and Marie was a different size, or I was sure they would have taken them too. Thank God, because I had eight hundred dollars in the pocket of my winter coat in one of the boxes. It was my emergency money, and I had saved and added to it for three years.

And this was the emergency I had been saving for.

I had less than four hundred left, but if I was careful, it would do me until my first check. I could eat a meal with every shift, which would save me money. Maybe I could bring the snack home. Ramen was cheap. The hotel was only about a twenty-minute walk. I could save on gas on nice days, although the thought of walking at two in the morning seemed a bit scary.

But again, it wasn't forever. I could make do.

I leaned back on the sofa with a sigh, suddenly overcome. I hadn't been able to relax once since this had happened. I was so glad I hadn't let Barry drive me to work that day—I would have lost my car as well. He had wanted to, but something made me say no and lie, telling him I had errands.

When it first happened, I didn't know what to do. I rented month-to-month and rent was coming due, and my landlord had zero problem kicking people out for nonpayment of rent.

A few days later, still unsure what to do, I was sitting in a coffee shop in Toronto when I heard two women discussing the hotel in Niagara Falls and the opportunities to work there. Curious, I leaned over and asked them about it, and they were happy to share their experience. *"I got on in the kitchen," one enthused. "I've been applying here for months and got nothing. The place is huge—four restaurants. I'm sure you could get something."* After they left, I checked out the hotel. I made the decision and put what few things I had left in the car and drove down to Niagara. The landlord was going to kick me out in short order anyway, so I figured I had nothing to lose.

And today had been a good day.

I had a job, a place to live, and I was safe.

A low voice, deep brown eyes, and wide shoulders came to mind. Mr. Ricci.

Aldo.

I'd seen his name on the forms I filled out. I recalled how I'd felt when I walked into his office and saw him.

Taken aback. He stood as I walked in, his presence filling the room. I felt a shiver race down my spine.

He was incredibly tall. Broad and muscular. He towered over me and, given my height, that was something. His eyes were a rich brown, and his hair was dark. His features were strong, and he had a cleft in his chin. He had an air of authority about him. His handshake was firm, his skin warm. He was intimidating, yet I wasn't afraid of him.

I wondered if I should be.

He'd also been kind. Directed me here. Assured me all the employees were looked after.

But I saw how he looked at me. The glimmer of desire in his eyes before he shut it down. He stared at my legs when the slit in my skirt opened a bit too far, his gaze lingering. He'd cleared his throat before speaking.

I found him very sexy. But he was one of the managers. Off-limits.

Still, I found him intriguing. He had an aloofness surrounding him. Was that real or a front he put on to keep people at arm's length?

I sighed as I looked around. I guessed I would find out tomorrow at the meet-and-greet.

There was a knock on the door, and I opened it. Fran stood there, smiling. "I thought you could use these until you're settled," she said, thrusting a small pile toward me. There was a pillow and blanket, as well as a couple of towels. "I know a good warehouse where you can buy necessities," she added. "Salvage, buyouts, that sort of thing. Good prices."

Her kindness was unexpected, and I had to blink at the surprising moisture in my eyes. "Thank you."

She nodded. "Our daughter is on her own too. I would like to think if she needed help, she would be offered it."

"I'll get these back to you as soon as I can."

"No rush, dear. I'm glad Mr. Ricci sent you our way. Brian and I like going to the casino, and he arranged a lovely night for our anniversary a few months ago. He is always kind to us. We were happy to help a friend of his."

I smiled. I was hardly a friend since I had only met him today, but I kept that to myself. "I'm glad he did as well. I'll be a good tenant."

She looked pleased. "I have no doubt. Now, if you need anything, we're number 101, all right?"

"Thank you."

She left, and I made up the sofa and got ready for bed. I was eager for tomorrow and getting into a schedule.

And if I was being truthful, getting another chance to see the mysterious Mr. Ricci.

I studied the menu, committing it to memory. It wasn't complicated. Sandwiches, burgers, soups, salads. Good, hearty fare—again, a nod to the fifties. Malts and milkshakes were featured, and I had to admit, my mouth watered reading the descriptions. I already decided I would have a Reuben and a vanilla shake for dinner.

I got ready and headed to the casino for the meet-and-greet. I wore my uniform, adding a belt and black sneakers. I wore my hair pushed back from my face with a scarf and put on some makeup.

I guessed there were about fifty people at the event. Cold and hot beverages were offered and even some finger food. I fixed a plate and took a cup of coffee, looking around the room. It was sumptuous and grand. I had a feeling everything in this hotel was top-notch.

I introduced myself to other newcomers, meeting a few more people who were going to be working at the Rolling Dice Deli. I had just put down my plate and wiped my mouth when I felt a shiver run down my spine. I turned slowly and met the gaze of Aldo Ricci. He was across the room with another man I assumed was Mr. Costas. He looked every inch the powerful tycoon I had heard he was. Tall, broad shoulders that tapered to a lean waist, and I was sure his suit cost more than my car. He had chestnut-colored hair and a stern expression on his face. Mr. Ricci said something to him, and he smiled, but even that looked stern. His expression was set to serious, and I had the feeling he didn't relax very often. Mr. Ricci was taller than him, bigger as well. Even across the room, I could see his muscles rippling under the tight sleeves of his jacket.

I made small talk with other people while watching them covertly. They stopped and spoke briefly with every person. Shook their hand. I noticed Mr. Ricci did most of the talking, but whoever they were greeting had their full attention until they moved on to the next person. It was classy and a nice touch. The last restaurant I worked at, I had never met the owner. Not once. I dealt with his manager only. It was a great move on their part here, meeting every person they hired. It made the job feel more…personal.

They came closer, and my breath caught in my throat. I saw the glances Mr. Costas was getting. He was incredibly handsome, and there was no doubt the broad, forbidding set of his shoulders and the stern expression were a striking combination. Combined with his obvious power and wealth, he drew a lot of attention. Which he ignored.

But it was Aldo—Mr. Ricci—who had my attention. He was big and broad. Powerful. He moved like a jungle cat, his gaze ever roaming, his body lithe and graceful for someone so large. It screamed sex to me, and I had to stop staring at him. But invariably, our eyes met and held more than once, his glance scorching. By the time they were in front of me, I was a mass of nerves. Mr. Ricci, however, was professional and courteous. Removed.

"Ms. Nelson. Nice to see you again," he said, then introduced me to Mr. Costas. "Roman Costas, Violet Nelson. She's joining the staff at Rolling Dice."

I shook Mr. Costas's hand. "Lovely to meet you. I look forward to working here."

"Already in your uniform, I see," he observed.

"My first shift is tonight."

"Welcome to the Maple."

He had a nice voice. Rich and smooth. Aldo's was rougher, lower. Their looks suited their voices.

"Have you known each other a long time?" I asked.

They both looked surprised at my question.

"Since we were kids," Aldo replied.

"Thought as much."

"Why is that?" Roman asked, looking genuinely curious.

"When you know someone well, it shows." I smiled at them. "You are very protective of your friend," I said to Aldo.

He smiled, his teeth white and straight. "Part of my job."

I tilted my head. "Part of your heart," I replied.

Their surprise turned into shock at my words and seemed to render them speechless. I wasn't sure if I had crossed a line or not, so I smiled and nodded at them. "Thank you for this. It was great to meet you."

I turned and walked away.

When I glanced over my shoulder, I was met with Aldo's intense gaze. It burned into me, flickering and bringing an unexpected reaction to my chest.

Desire.

I shook my head and headed to the deli.

Desire I would never act on. I needed this job.

I doubted I would see much of him anyway.

Right?

CHAPTER 4
ALDO

I watched her leave, taking with her some of the heat I felt when we were close.

"Observant," Roman muttered. "She is a clever one. Maybe dangerous."

I nodded. "She is."

"She from here?"

"No, just moved down from Toronto." I glanced his way, careful to keep my voice neutral. "We don't usually go for staff."

He laughed. "Not interested. But I liked her. Direct." He grinned. "She certainly wears that uniform well."

She looked incredible in the uniform. The shirt hugged her breasts like a lover, the pants skimming her curves perfectly. I liked the scarf and the belt. I liked everything about the outfit. Especially the woman wearing it. But I couldn't say that.

"Yep."

He looked at me. "You all right?"

"I'm fine."

He looked toward the door and back at me, then chuckled. "Okay. Let's finish this off. I have a ton of paperwork on my desk."

We finished working the room and headed back to the office. Roman was in a contemplative mood. "Lots of new hires."

I looked up from the file I was working on. "Always are in this business. Turnover is high with staff in the hospitality sector."

"How can we keep the good ones?" he asked, turning his chair and staring out the window at the Falls. He loved looking at the water.

"I think we do well. Our turnover is lower than most. We pay a high wage, we give them benefits, make sure they're protected. We have zero complaints, no harassment issues. Our staff is well treated."

"That woman," he mused.

"Woman?"

"The tall one. Violet. She seems intelligent. Observant. How long will she be happy being a waitress?"

"I have no idea. It was the job she applied for. She has experience."

He turned. "She'd be great in the formal dining room. She would rock the uniform. Those long legs in a tux? Or as a dealer. Imagine the crowds around her table."

For some reason, his observation pissed me off. "She does seem intelligent. One of the reasons we have such a great record with employees is we don't exploit them. She has no interest in being a dealer or working the Skyview," I said, referring to the formal, members-only dining room. "She asked for the deli, I gave it to her. If she requests a transfer, then I'll handle it. Until then, leave her alone. In fact, leave her alone completely, Roman. She isn't your type, and I don't need to lose someone I think will be a good fit because you want to know how those legs feel wrapped around your ass as you fuck her. Find someone else."

He stared at me and burst out laughing.

"I never thought about those legs that way, Aldo. But I think you have."

I stood.

"Fuck off."

His laughter followed me out of the door.

I got in my car and took a drive. Roman stared at the Falls to calm himself. I drove. I wound away from the Falls and into the park, pulling over in a secluded spot and parking. I walked to an empty bench and tugged off my jacket. I sat, stretching out my legs and crossing my ankles. I drew in some long breaths and rolled my shoulders, letting the sun and quiet do their job. After a few moments, I felt better. I ignored the buzzing of my phone and concentrated on the peace. The park would be busier soon, with tourists and locals flocking to the area for picnics and fun, but right now, it was fairly deserted.

My phone buzzed again, and I answered it.

"Roman."

"I was pulling your leg, Aldo."

"Is that a fact?"

"I saw how you looked at that woman. I wanted to see how you reacted. I was right."

"The subject is not up for discussion. She is an employee."

"We don't have a nonfraternization clause."

"I am her boss's boss. That is an HR issue screaming to happen."

"But you like her."

"I don't know her."

"You still like her."

"Unless you need me, I'm on a break."

"A break?" he laughed. "That's a first."

"Do you need something?"

"No."

I hung up. He would hate that, but he deserved it.

And he was right. I liked her.

What a fucking complication.

On my way back to the hotel, I stopped by the apartment building Violet was now living in. Brian and Fran were outside, tidying the yard. The building was well maintained, and I knew they took great pride in it.

Brian shook my hand.

"Thank you for helping Ms. Nelson."

He waved me off. "She seems great. A bit down on her luck."

Fran shook her head. "I took her some linens and a pillow last night. She was just going to sleep on the sofa with nothing."

I didn't like that idea. For some reason, the thought of her being without bothered me.

"Thank you." I reached into my pocket and handed Brian some cash. "First and last."

"We can wait."

"No. When she tries to pay, tell her it is handled. I'll speak with her." I paused. "But don't say anything to her right away."

They exchanged a glance but said nothing. Brian handed Fran the cash. "You can record that, hon."

She took the money and went inside. I shook Brian's hand again. "Next time you're coming for a night, let me know. I'll get you a table at the buffet on the house." They loved the buffet.

"Thanks, Aldo."

"If Ms. Nelson needs anything, let me know."

He nodded. "I will."

The next night, I was tired. The casino was packed, the noise level growing increasingly louder as the hours wore on. Laughter, conversation, the machines, the crowds. All of it swelled, rarely dying down. The casino was always busy, but the weekends in the summer were the craziest. Tourists, locals, and VIPs poured through the doors constantly. And Saturday evenings were the busiest of them all. Roman and I had been walking, shaking hands, overseeing any issues, helping to set up private games, doing everything we needed to do to make sure our VIPs were happy. They spent a huge amount of money here. It was obscene.

We also made sure the regular people simply enjoying a night out were satisfied. Drinks, snacks, upgraded food, complimentary parking. I issued it all, knowing a few free things and some preferential treatment would bring their hard-earned dollars back again. The hotel was booked solid as well, although I knew some of the rooms would barely be used. Many of the serious gamblers wouldn't leave the casino until the early hours of the morning, or even later.

I glanced at my watch, not surprised to see it was past midnight. I was hungry and needed a break. Normally, I would order something and head to my office, but tonight, I found myself outside Rolling Dice. It was quieter but still busy. I stood for a moment and watched, my gaze focused on one thing.

Violet Nelson.

Today, she wore the uniform with the polka-dot skirt and the tight T-shirt. It left her legs bare, and even in sneakers, they were sexy as hell. She moved around the tables, filling coffee cups, taking orders, carrying a tray like a pro. Wanda saw me and came over. "Mr. Ricci."

"How is she doing?" I asked, trying to appear casual.

"She is a godsend. She showed up early last night, menu memorized. I showed her around and explained the software, and an hour later, you'd think she'd been here a month. The cooks love her, the other staff think she is great, and the customers agree. Her tips are amazing." Wanda laughed softly. "She tried to give some back last night because she thought there was a mistake. Even with the kitchen portion taken out, her tips were bigger than anyone's. I suspect it will happen again tonight."

I nodded, secretly pleased.

"Good."

"You want a table?"

"In the staff section." I didn't want to be disturbed for a bit.

"You want the usual?"

"Please."

"You know where it is."

I walked to the back, around a corner that provided some privacy. There were two booths and, at present, both were empty. I slid into one, removing my jacket and rolling up my sleeves.

A moment later, Wanda set down a vanilla milkshake in front of me. "Sandwich is coming right up."

"Thanks."

I sipped the cold shake, the sweet drink refreshing and delicious. We had the best milkshakes around. I shut my eyes, relaxing, waiting for my sandwich.

A few moments later, there was a noise as another staff member came around the corner.

"Oh."

Somehow I recognized her from that one breathy sound. I opened my eyes and met the hazel gaze of Violet Nelson. Before I could speak, Wanda came in and slid my plate in front of me. She looked between Violet and me and laughed. "Twins." Then she left.

I glanced at Violet's tray and chuckled. We both had a Reuben sandwich and fries. A vanilla shake. She began to head to the other table, and for some reason, I held up my hand. "Join me."

She slipped in, and I picked up my sandwich, taking a large bite. The hot corned beef and tangy sauerkraut hit my tastebuds, and I groaned. "Damn."

Violet laughed, following suit, although her bite was much smaller. "I think they make the best Reuben around. I had it last night too."

"I agree. Try the clubhouse, though. Or the burger."

She grinned, taking a sip of her shake. "If I eat this way every night, I'll have to jog to work."

I stopped, the sandwich partway to my mouth. "You aren't walking, are you? With the shift you're working?"

"Oh no. I drive." She smiled. "It is very generous of you to give us such great parking rates."

I shrugged, relieved. "We try to think of what people need. We want our employees to be happy." I took a sip of my shake. "Wanda says you're a rock star."

She laughed. "It's a great place. People are happy for the most part, the food is good, the other staff are nice." She yawned. "I have to get used to the hours. But I'll be fine." She bit and chewed, swallowing her sandwich and eating some fries that she doused in ketchup. "Speaking of which, thank you for the help with the apartment."

"You settle in all right?"

She laughed dryly. "I opened my cases. Luckily, there was a sofa there, so I'm fine."

I wondered why I disliked the word fine so much. I pretended not to know anything and finished my sandwich. "You need a couple pieces of furniture?"

She frowned. "Pardon?"

"We replace stuff all the time. We just renovated an entire floor. We have a bunch of dressers, tables, chairs. You can take your pick."

She eyed me suspiciously. "I don't take charity."

I loved her independence. Her refusal to show any pity for her situation.

"We always let staff get things first. Then we donate the rest."

It was a bit of a lie. We did donate.

"Oh. I could use a dresser, I guess."

"Okay. You want to pick?"

"No, I just need some drawer space."

"Fine. I'll have one dropped off."

"Um, maybe a lamp if you have one? I like to read, and the only light in the place is an overhead."

"Yep. Plenty of those."

She finished her sandwich and stood. "Thank you, Mr. Ricci."

"You're welcome, Ms. Nelson."

"My friends call me Vi."

I smiled ruefully. "You have to call me Mr. Ricci."

"I know."

Then she leaned down and kissed my cheek. It was fast, unexpected. Soft and sweet. "Thank you, Aldo," she whispered.

"You're welcome…Vi."

We stared at each other. There was no disguising the heat between us. It was a living, breathing thing. My fingers twitched with the need to touch her. My body yearned to feel her close. As close as I could get her.

Before I could give in to my impulses, she grabbed her plate and left.

I stared after her, amused by her forwardness, and holding my cheek.

Why, I wasn't sure.

Except I was smiling.

Then I picked up her milkshake and finished it.

I was sure it was sweeter because her lips had touched the same straw.

Except, that was crazy and impossible.

Right?

CHAPTER 5
ALDO

"That one." I looked around. "That lamp." I pointed to a particularly nice chair. It looked like the one in my private suite, only smaller. "Add that too."

Every floor of the hotel had a different style, different furnishings. The farther you went up in the building, the more lavish it became. Roman insisted on the best, no matter what floor it was, and he employed a crew that did nothing but inspect the rooms and change furniture and fixtures if they became damaged or tired-looking. Everything was maintained to be top-notch. We did recycle some of the more extravagant pieces to the lower floors, so they, too, looked high-end. We donated a lot, clearing out the storage area at least once a year. I made sure to pick nice, comfortable, top-quality pieces for her. Violet.

"Anything else, boss?"

"No. Deliver it this afternoon. Brian will let you in." I handed a slip of paper to Josh. "Make sure it happens."

He nodded. "I'll look after it myself."

I headed upstairs, satisfied. I had helped Vi. Violet. *Ms. Nelson.*

She had a place to live, some furniture, and a job.

I could move on. Stop thinking about her.

In the office, I sat down, pouring a cup of coffee. Lunch with Nonna the day before had been its usual treat. The woman cooked all our favorites, and I had taken home leftovers. Always a bonus.

I scanned some reports, pleased at the dollar figures I saw. Roman would be happy as well.

He walked in, looking tired. He was an insomniac a lot of the time. It had started in his later teen years when his father would be on the prowl at night, ready to spring one of his surprises on the boys. It continued after his father died, and at times, I worried over his health. He grabbed naps, a few hours of sleep after roaming the casino at night. He told me he slept better at his estate, but given his schedule, he was here far more than he was there. Nonna nagged him all the time, but he never changed his ways.

He sat down heavily.

"You were at the estate. Did you not sleep at all?"

He waved his hand. "Too much on my mind. I'll grab a few hours later before the crowds hit tonight."

"Sleep is required for a strong body and mind."

"Thanks, Mom," he replied, his sarcasm evident.

The door opened and Luca came in, his expression neutral, his demeanor curiously subdued. He looked a little tired, which was unusual for him.

Roman and I exchanged a look.

"How was your weekend?" I asked lightly.

"I babysat the princess all weekend." Luca sat down, reaching for the coffee. "I told her I was in meetings all day today. She's at the spa at the Maple." He glared at Roman. "You're paying for a whole pampering day."

"Is she that bad?"

Luca leaned his head back. "I thought so at first," he admitted. "I took her to all the places her brother insisted she wanted to go to. Mostly shopping. She seemed to be the empty-headed princess I thought her to be."

Another glance happened between Roman and me.

"Then last night, we talked. Actually talked. She told me she had done enough of the list her brother had put together. She told me what she really wanted to do." He paused, taking a drink of coffee. "I hafta admit, I was surprised."

"Like what?"

A glimmer of a smile tugged his mouth. "She wants to go bowling. To a movie. She's never had a taco. She just wants to do some fun things. Her father and brother are so overprotective, her life is mapped out for her. She adores them but hates their control." He ran his hand over his chin. "She has an idea what they are involved in but not the depth of it. She gets frustrated being kept on such a short lead. She hated me because of what I represented. I felt the same way." He was quiet for a moment. "She isn't the airhead her brother thinks she is. She's well-read and funny. Smart."

"You like her," Roman stated.

Luca frowned and stood, no longer subdued. "I'm tolerating her. Trying to find common ground. She's here all week, so I have to waste more of my time escorting her around. You owe me."

Roman frowned. "I thought she was going back today."

"She decided to stay."

"And you offered to keep showing her around?" I asked, trying not to laugh.

Luca glared. “To keep peace.” He shook his head. “Fuckers.” He strode to the door. “I’m going to get some food then I want to meet in your office, Roman. We have business to discuss. I don’t have time to gossip over a pretty girl with you like some old ladies.”

He slammed the door behind him, and I grinned. Even Roman looked amused.

“Keeping the peace? I call BS on that one,” I observed.

“He called her a pretty girl. He’s taking her bowling. Luca hates bowling.” Roman sat back. “I think my brother protests too much. He’s pissed off because he dislikes liking her.”

“I think you’re right.” I rubbed my chin. “This could be interesting.”

He nodded, looking thoughtful. “I think so as well.”

The next few days passed, life as busy as always. I worked in the office, walked the floor, met with people. Sat with Roman. Escorted him to some meetings. He had a personal bodyguard, but I went with him to a lot of meetings outside the casino. And every one that happened inside. He trusted me implicitly. Often, he went on his own to his estate, but it was well guarded and secure and his car bulletproof.

Although he and Luca had changed their ways of doing things, cutting ties with the old, forming new alliances, danger still lurked. Roman remained a figurehead within the syndicate, controlling the Niagara region. Luca handled the Greater Toronto Area, and he was far more visible and more involved. They were heavily into legalized drugs, owning several of the marijuana grow farms and legal stores in the region. But they also double-dipped, selling undeclared plants to the hundreds of stores now retailing the product. It was a delicate balance, but Luca did it well. They refused to handle hard drugs some others in the syndicate dealt with. The brothers also liked art and found huge profits in smuggling it. Still illegal, but their piece of the pie was less violent and bloody than their father's history within the organization. It was also more profitable.

I knew, if he could, Roman would wash his hands of all of it and concentrate on his hotels and casinos. But because of his loyalty to Luca, he stayed involved. I had seen his desire for that life waning, growing more distant as time passed. I wondered at times how long it would be before he wanted a complete separation.

His father would roll over in his grave. I hope he knew and that he suffered.

I signed off on some comp orders and handed them to the front desk manager. "They're potential big spenders. Make them feel special."

Maurice nodded. "Will do."

Without thought, my feet took me past the entrance to Rolling Dice. I'd found myself around there a lot the past while. I scanned the restaurant, my body tightening as Vi came into view. She wore the black pants today. They hugged her ass and legs like a second skin. Instead of a belt, she had a bright scarf wrapped around her waist, and her hair was slicked back, her makeup on point. She looked every inch a sassy, perky, sexy waitress. I covertly watched her then stepped back before she could see me. I hated that other men saw her that way, and I hated that I hated it.

I headed to the casino, cursing myself. I needed to stop, yet I seemed unable to do so. If Roman found out, he'd rag me relentlessly. He was already enjoying Luca's situation far too much.

I shook my head as I walked the floor, my gaze sweeping the room constantly. The machines were busy, people everywhere, and the night was young. Staff were carrying drinks, helping customers. The deeper I walked into the casino, the calmer it became. The private elevator led to the second floor. That was where the real gambling happened. The games, the heavy hitters. The farther you went, the more opulent the rooms became. It was discreet, quiet, and soaked in money. Power. We called it The Epicenter.

Everything was prepared for the evening. Private poker games were set up. The high-roller room was ready, everything in place and perfect. The floors gleamed. The view of the Falls from the all-glass curved window at the end was spectacular. It was one only the privileged few witnessed. There was no way to access it aside from this room, so there were never any gawkers or curious onlookers. Bulletproof glass and a film on the outside ensured total privacy for those within, those with the deep pockets and the connections to get in here. The minimum bid to get into these games was an average person's take-home pay for a year. Sometimes more.

This was Roman's domain. Here, he was king. A nod of his head gave you more credit. A simple tilt of his chin could exclude you from ever setting foot in here again. Having a drink with him was akin to rubbing elbows with God. Men were jealous of him. Women wanted him. He ignored them all, for the most part.

I walked beside him nightly, his constant shadow. On the nights he was absent, it was me who dispensed the permission. Made the decisions. The power was addictive, and you had to be careful not to let it go to your head. You left your emotions at the door and let your brain do the thinking. Nothing else. This was a business, and that was how we ran it. We had seen too many others fail.

That was unacceptable.

Satisfied all was perfect, I headed to my office. I ordered a sandwich and coffee, resisting the temptation to go to the deli. I had to stop thinking about Vi.

When I heard the quiet knock, I called out for the person bringing me my meal to come in.

But it wasn't just anyone. It was Vi. She walked in, holding a tray, and I frowned. "What are you doing here, and why do you have my food?" I began to stand, feeling anger surge through me. "Did you transfer? Were you not happy?"

She blinked at my tone, then laughed. "Relax, big man. I was walking this way and saw Angie bringing the tray. I told her I'd take it for you since I was coming to see you." She slid it onto my desk. "I'm perfectly happy at the deli." Then she tsked. "You should have ordered from there."

I sat down and chuckled. "I just need something fast." I picked up my sandwich, trying not to stare at her. I did startle as she picked up the coffee carafe and poured it into my cup. She slid it my way, then sat down.

"What can I help you with?" I asked, my voice gruff.

"I tried to give Brian the first month's rent, and he said I had been taken care of. I was wondering what you might know of that. He mentioned last was covered as well." She crossed her legs, swinging one foot in agitation and readying herself for a fight.

I couldn't resist teasing her. "What makes you think I had anything to do with it?"

She rolled her eyes and tossed her head. It was sexy the way her hair clung to her head, and the black eyeliner she wore emphasized the movement of her eyes. "As if anyone else would. You got me in there. It only makes sense, but I told you I don't take charity."

Luckily, I was prepared.

"Yes, I paid first and last." I held up my hand before she could rain hellfire on me. "On behalf of the casino. There will be withdrawals coming off your check to repay the loan. Small enough it won't put you in a bad position financially."

She didn't believe me. She pursed her lips, and her foot began swinging again. I imagined she was mentally picturing kicking my balls.

I picked up the phone and pressed an extension.

"Accounting. Eleanor here," a female voice answered.

"Eleanor, it's Mr. Ricci. The matter I spoke to you about the other day. Has it been set in place?"

"The wage adjustment to repay the loan for"—there was some shuffling of papers—"Violet Nelson? Yes, sir. Taken care of."

"Thank you."

I hung up and met her eyes. They were lovely—even angry and frustrated. Her emotions brought a rosy hue to her cheeks, which suited her.

"This seems unorthodox."

I shrugged, secretly loving her spirit but determined to win this. "We are not your usual employers, I agree. We take care of our people." Then, just to anger her further, I added more fuel to the fire. "Your furniture will be there when you get home from work this evening. I added a chair."

She blew out a breath, and I was sure she wanted to say something, but she stood. "Thank you, Mr. Ricci. I appreciate the kindness. You are very generous."

She paused at the door. "And you aren't the only one watching…*Aldo*. I have eyes too." She smiled. "Enjoy your sandwich."

And she left.

I sat back, once again amused by her lack of filter and feistiness.

I wondered what would happen if she found out there was no loan to be repaid. I had arranged with Eleanor to take extra tax off her checks but list it as a separate line with an odd code. Violet would actually get that money back when she did her taxes. I assumed by the time that happened, she would have left the deli and gone on to a better, more long-term job and wouldn't think twice about it.

No doubt forgotten about me as well.

I dropped my sandwich, no longer hungry.

VI

It was well past two when I got back to my apartment. I was tired. It had been a busy night. I stopped for a moment, confused, then recalled that Aldo said he'd had furniture delivered here.

I ran my hand over the tall dresser, checked out the light and was pleased with the chair he had sent. It was a wingback and, as everything in the hotel was, the colors of the Falls. White, gray, blue, turquoise—everywhere you looked, you saw the ever-changing water. The chair was gray and blue, in almost new condition, and the perfect spot to read or watch TV. Not that I had one.

Exhausted, I got ready and lay on the sofa, falling asleep quickly. In the morning, I made coffee and spent some time moving things around until I was satisfied. I had been to the salvage place a few times and had the essentials now. A coffeemaker, a couple of pans, a cookie sheet, and my own bedding. The dollar store provided lots of the little things. Plates, cups, glasses, utensils, and other sundries. I only bought two of most things, since I highly doubted I would be throwing dinner parties, but it was nice to have a spare plate. I had taken some rolled posters from advertisements they changed all the time at the deli that Wanda said I could have. I hung them on the walls so the place didn't seem so bare. The pictures were views of the Falls, and they looked bright and pretty. I didn't want to do much since I had no idea how long I would be staying, but as I looked around, I felt good. It was small, but it was mine.

I pried up the loose floorboard and pulled out the flat box I had brought home from the casino. I counted my tip money, shocked. Some nights, I pulled in over three hundred dollars in cash. Most nights, it was at least two hundred. And I saw the total of tip money that would be added to my next check from credit card sales. My first priority had been to pay the first and last month's rent, but it seemed that had happened already.

I stared at the money, bundling it back into the box and hiding it back under the loose floorboard. The new wingback chair sat over it, so you didn't notice it.

I poured another coffee and sat on the sofa. I knew I should look at buying a decent bed, but I was holding off. The sofa was comfortable enough for now. I could afford it, especially since I didn't have the huge cash outlay of the rent, but I was going to wait a bit.

Aldo drifted into my mind again. He'd looked weary yesterday when I went to see him. For some reason, it bothered me to see him at his desk, eating a sandwich alone. Why, I had no idea.

I had noticed him several times while I worked. Striding across the front lobby, sometimes beside Mr. Costas, other times on his own. A few times, I saw him look into the restaurant as if he were looking for something, but Wanda said he often came in to make sure everything was okay. I had to admit, I was a little disappointed. A small part hoped he was looking for me.

Even yesterday, I saw how his gaze lingered on me. It was so intense, it felt as if he were burning my image into his head. I know I stared at him. He was handsome in a rugged, manly way. But when he spoke, his voice was calm and detached, and I wondered if I had imagined the heat I felt.

When I had impulsively kissed his cheek last week, his skin was smooth and warm under my lips. His scent, woodsy and clean, hit me, filling my head. He had looked startled but not angry. I could smell him again yesterday, sitting across the desk, the aroma pleasant and warm. His explanation about the money was acceptable, yet I still had the lingering feeling there was more to it than he was saying.

Mr. Ricci had many layers, I decided, and he hid his true self very well. I wasn't stupid. I recognized who Roman Costas was—and the fact that he wasn't simply a hotel/casino owner. That meant Aldo was as deep into illegal activities as Roman was since he was his right hand. But I also had a feeling there was more to both of them, aside from money and power. Everyone I spoke to had nothing but positive things to say about the men. How great they were to work for. I realized some might be naïve and not know they were syndicate men, but they were still respected and admired. There was a lot to be said about that.

At times, there was something in Aldo's expression. His voice. I had a feeling there was more to him than people knew. I thought that protective instinct he had for Roman would blanket all those he cared for. And God forbid you crossed him. He would be lethal.

I shivered thinking about what he would be like in bed. All that power and simmering emotion he kept bottled up escaping. How his mouth would feel on mine. The control he would assert. My nipples tightened, and I felt an ache between my legs simply thinking about it.

I shook my head and stood. I would never get a chance to find out. But that didn't stop the thoughts that washed over me.

Or my fingers playing with my clit in the shower, groaning out Aldo's name as I orgasmed.

Twice.

CHAPTER 6
ALDO

The following Monday, Roman and I crossed the floor of the main entrance, our strides slower than normal. He was looking everywhere, covertly checking on every detail. He demanded perfection, insisting the lobby was the first impression for his clientele and he wanted it to astonish.

The illuminated fountain erupted, the water cascading over the layers of glass and crystals, the lights dancing under the flow of water. The glass dome at the top glittered in the sunlight, adding to the spectacle. It was mesmerizing and one of my favorite things in the lobby. Patrons and staff loved it. The floors gleamed, the surfaces free of dust and fingerprints. The front desk was busy, the people checking in being dealt with in a courteous, efficient manner. Everything looked good, right down to the station Roman insisted on for guests. Cold water, hot coffee and tea, plus small snacks were available to all guests twenty-four seven. The area was checked constantly and was located next to the concierge's desk to make sure stragglers didn't wander in and have a feast.

Roman nodded, pleased, his pace picking up. We were headed toward the casino, when his steps faltered, and he muttered a curse. "Fuck."

I followed his gaze, seeing Mason Miller striding across the lobby, his expression dark and angry.

Roman rolled his shoulders as if preparing for a fight. I cleared my throat. "We're in public right now."

"I'm aware."

Mason stopped in front of Roman, two men behind him. "Where the fuck is my sister?"

Roman tilted his head, studying him. "I think you forget who you're speaking to," he said softly, the undercurrent to his voice clear.

Mason narrowed his eyes but lowered his voice and injected a respectful tone. Smart man.

"Hello, Roman. How are you?"

"I'm good. What brings you to *my city*?" he said, emphasizing the fact that Mason was within his territory.

“I’m trying to locate my rogue sister.”

Roman frowned. “The last time I spoke with him, Luca said she was heading home on the weekend.”

“She didn’t come home. She left me a voice mail, saying she’d let me know her schedule when she had made up her mind. I haven’t been able to get hold of her since.”

“And you came to me because…? Shouldn’t you be in touch with Luca and in Toronto?”

Mason held up his phone. “She hasn’t returned my calls. Nor has your brother. My tracker shows me she is here. It was turned off Saturday, and when it came to life this morning, it showed her in *this* hotel.” He stepped forward, lowering his voice. “If your brother is fucking with my sister, I *will* end him.”

Roman grunted. “You might have to get in line.”

Roman glanced at me, and I headed to the front desk, getting Maurice to pull up the information I needed. “Did Luca check in to his suite this weekend?”

“No. It shows empty. But…”

“But?” I asked.

“I saw him here early Sunday. It slipped my mind until later, and I checked but saw his suite wasn’t being used. However, when I was going through reports earlier, I saw his credit card.”

"So he checked in to a different room and is paying for it?" I was confused.

"I believe so. I wasn't at the desk. I doubt the younger staff would have recognized him."

"What room?"

He tapped the screen, and I read it, my eyes widening. "Is he still there?"

"It is booked until Wednesday."

"Thank you."

I strode back to Roman.

"Is he here?" Roman inquired. "He isn't answering his phone."

"Yes."

"Take Mason to my office. I'll go find Luca, and we'll clear this up."

"A word," I said quietly.

With a frown, Roman stepped to the side, his gaze angry. "What the hell is going on?"

"I think I should go get him."

"Why?"

"Luca checked in to another room—not his suite."

"Why would he do that?"

I glanced at Mason, who was watching us, his gaze dark and intense. I angled myself so he couldn't see Roman's face.

"He checked in to the honeymoon suite, Roman. And he isn't alone."

Roman's eyebrows shot up. "*Holy fuck.*"

Roman escorted Mason to the private office on the top floor, deciding it might be best if I fetched Luca. Mason's men stayed on the main floor.

The upstairs office wasn't a place Roman usually brought anyone outside his circle, but I had a feeling he knew this wasn't going to be pretty. Extra bodies were not welcome. Surprisingly, Mason didn't argue.

I went to the honeymoon suite to fetch Luca. I hoped he would tell Mason that his sister was still in Toronto and he was here with someone else. I prayed to God he hadn't lost her. Or even worse, was in the honeymoon suite with her. I wasn't sure I had enough bullets in my gun to protect him and Roman.

My hopes were dashed when Luca opened the door wearing nothing but a robe and a scowl. Following behind him, a woman I recognized from a picture I had seen. She was average height, with golden-brown hair, dark eyes, and a pretty smile. Attractive and intelligent-looking. But at the moment, she was looking disheveled and tired. The entirely wrong kind of tired right now.

"What the hell are you doing here, Aldo?"

I indicated the woman behind him. "Mason is here. Looking for her."

She gasped, leaving me in no doubt that she was Justine. Luca grimaced. "*Fuck.* I thought we had more time."

"He's in Roman's office. You need to come now." I paused. "Or, once you're dressed."

He shut his eyes. "Give us ten minutes."

"I'll wait."

"I know my way."

"I am not walking into that office without her. Mason is beyond pissed and trigger-happy. I am not getting my balls shot off so you can play hide the salami with a princess."

"Hey," Luca snapped. "Show my wife some respect."

I gaped at him.

His wife?

Holy shit, this was worse than I thought.

"I'll wait."

I opened the office door, walking in first. Behind me, Luca held Justine's hand firmly in his. Roman and Mason were already standing, glasses of scotch in their hands. Mason looked between Luca and Justine, fury in his glance.

"If you have fucked around with my sister, I will end you." He slammed his empty glass down on Roman's desk. "I will kill all of you."

Before I could speak, Justine did. "Oh relax, Mason. Do you ever get tired of blowing smoke? No one is killing anyone."

Roman focused his attention on Luca. "Explain. You said she was going home this weekend. Why is she here, with you, in my hotel, and why isn't she answering her brother's calls?"

Again, Justine spoke, directing her words to her brother. "*She* is perfectly capable of speaking. I had my phone off because I went over the border for the night, Mason. I didn't want you interrupting my time away. And you can direct your questions to me, Roman. I know my brother thinks I'm an airhead, but I can actually speak and think for myself."

Luca chuckled, pulling her close and pressing a kiss to her head. "That's my girl."

Mason growled, going for his weapon, but I pulled out my gun, shaking my head. "Let's not start something we'll all regret. Let the lady speak."

"Thank you, Aldo."

I didn't respond, but I felt a grudging respect for her. I was worried, though, that I would have to use my gun when she told him her real news.

"Why did you go over the border? I never gave you permission to leave the country," Mason raged. He glared at Luca. "What the hell were you thinking, allowing her?"

Luca shook his head. "I don't *allow* your sister anything. She is her own person. A fully grown woman capable of making her own decisions. You should really get to know her. She is amazing."

Roman was staring at Luca in disbelief. Luca's next words almost sent him over the edge. His normally stoic face went pale in shock.

"I took Justine to Vegas. We got married."

No one in the room moved. Even blinked. Luca kept talking. "My wife said she'd always wanted to see the Falls, so once we were married, we flew here and I got the honeymoon suite. Best view in the city. I was surprised to find it empty, but I took advantage. I was sure you wouldn't mind the business, brother." He winked at Roman as if all this was a joke.

A very bad one.

Roman was the first to speak. "You…got…*married*."

"Yes."

"To Justine."

"Yes."

"You've known her less than two weeks."

Luca smiled. "I couldn't bear the thought of letting her go."

"Last time we spoke, you could barely tolerate each other."

Luca shrugged. "I got to know the real woman."

Mason spoke directly to Justine, fury and ice dripping from his tone. "You're going home with me today."

"No, I'm not."

"Yes, you are. We'll get this farce annulled, and no one will be the wiser."

Justine crossed her arms. "Too late for an annulment."

Mason's angry expression turned lethal. His hand moved toward his weapon again, and I tutted, shaking my head in warning. "Leave those hands where I can see them. I'll shoot you even with your sister in the room."

"I'd let you," she scoffed, straightening her shoulders. "I'm not going anywhere."

Luca gripped her arms. "I'm not letting you take my wife."

Mason barked out an angry laugh. "You won't have a choice. I'm going to kill you."

Justine shook her head, stepping in front of Luca. "You hurt him, you hurt me. And I will never forgive you, Mason."

He stared at her. "You were supposed to come for a weekend of museums and galleries."

She laughed. "Those were your picks. I did them to please you. Luca took me everywhere I really wanted to go. Listened to me talk. Encouraged me to follow my dreams. I love him, Mason. With everything in me. I know it's fast, but it's real. I am staying here. With my husband. Now, you can either accept it or fight it. If you fight it, I will never speak to you again."

He stared, shell-shocked. "Father, Mother…"

"Will have to accept it. I'm not leaving."

He seemed to recover from his shock. "You'll do as I tell you—"

Luca cut him off, shifting Justine behind him and glaring. "You will speak to my wife with respect and remember you no longer have control over her. She is her own person, and I will protect her choices. I will protect her."

"This is war."

Roman stepped out from behind his desk. "Or is this love?" he said quietly. "I have never known Luca to act with anything but respect and clear thinking. He must love your sister a great deal to put aside responsibility and rational thinking to marry her."

"I do love her. She makes me happy."

An icy silence descended, every person in the room frozen, unsure of the next step. It was as if we were waiting for a sign to start.

"Was it the bowling?" I asked, trying to lighten the room.

Luca laughed, Roman joining him. Mason looked confused, and Justine shook her head in amusement. Roman indicated for me to lower my weapon. I did so but didn't put it away. I was worried about the vein throbbing in Mason's head.

"It was *her*," Luca replied, looking down at his wife with a tender expression. "She saw Luca. I saw Justine. That was all that mattered."

Mason stared at them, his shoulders bowing in defeat.

"Father will not accept a Vegas wedding."

"Then we'll get married again. Here. But nothing is changing the fact that we are legally married now. She is mine." Luca slid a possessive arm around Justine, pulling her close. "I will not let her go."

Mason dropped his head, shaking it in sorrow. "Why didn't *you* take her to the galleries, Roman? I knew she'd be safe with you. You have no appeal to most people."

Roman threw back his head in amusement, and I grinned. It was true. Unless he wanted you to like him, Roman couldn't give a shit about your opinion. He'd had zero interest in playing babysitter for Mason, and by turning the job over to Luca, he had set them on their path.

Roman approached Luca, holding out his hand. "Congratulations, big brother." He smiled kindly at Justine. "Welcome to the family." He looked nonplussed as she hugged him. He wasn't used to people touching him, but he accepted it, albeit awkwardly.

Mason sighed. "We need to talk." He looked at Justine. "Alone."

Luca bristled, but Justine nodded. "It's fine. We'll go to the suite."

Roman smiled, his expression neutral. "Aldo will escort you."

I knew he wanted me outside the door in case there was trouble. Mason didn't refuse—he didn't dare.

Roman turned to Luca. "It will give us a chance to talk as well."

I had a feeling more shouting would happen before the talking, but I opened the door and let Mason walk out ahead of me. Justine paused and lifted herself up on her toes to kiss Luca. "See you soon."

"I'm here if you need me."

She smiled at him so widely, even I felt her affection. "I know."

Luca appeared about half an hour later, striding down thc hall. He was upright and I didn't see any marks on him, so I assumed he and Roman had been actually talking, not trading fisticuffs. He paused. "All okay in there?" He indicated the closed door I had been guarding.

I nodded. "There were raised voices a couple of times, but nothing drastic." I had to grin. "Your woman wasn't taking any BS from her brother. She is feisty."

"She is incredible," he agreed. "So intelligent and curious. Her brother and father have no idea of the woman they've been keeping wrapped up. They're so busy trying to shield her, they're taking away her spirit." He shook his head. "She's very close to her mother and aunt and her female cousins. And she has several friends. She'll miss them, but she wants to be here with me. She'll give all that up to be with me, even knowing everything I'm involved with. I plan on letting her fly. I want to watch her soar. I think it will be incredible to watch."

I clapped him on the shoulder. "Congratulations." I paused. "Roman handling it all right?"

He smiled. "He's fine. He's over the shock. Once I deal with Mason, I'm taking her to meet Nonna. I think she'll love her."

I held out my hand. "I wish you all the best."

He smiled and shook my proffered palm. "Thanks, Aldo."

"Do you want me to stay?"

"No. I'll deal with Mason now. He loves Justine, and he wouldn't do anything stupid."

I slid my hand into my pocket and handed Luca the bullets I'd insisted Mason remove from his gun. "A little extra insurance."

He laughed and put them in his pocket. "I'm certain Justine has worked her magic by now, but thanks."

He went inside, and I headed up to Roman. He was at his desk, another glass of scotch at his elbow. I met his eyes and took a fresh glass, pouring a splash into the tumbler and taking a sip.

"Well, that was interesting."

He sat back. "I'm still processing." He shook his head. "Luca. Level-headed, always in control, never settling down, Luca. Married. To a woman he has known for an instant."

"Stranger things have happened."

"I'm aware." He took a sip of scotch. "He says the day he picked her up from the spa, they went for dinner at Maple II, and she got a little drunk and started talking about everything. Her life. Her family. She told him when she was sixteen, she was grabbed off the street on the way home from school. She was smart and managed to get away, but after that, her father and brother were relentless with security. Even when they found the people involved, they never let up. She's been chafing at the bit to get away. I asked him if he was sure she didn't see him as the escape, but he says no. And he is in love. *Fuck*, is he in love." He shook his head. "I have never heard him talk about someone the way he talks about her. She fascinates him. He admitted they haven't been apart since that night. He never wants to be without her again."

"So, what happens now?"

"He's going with her to meet her parents and face the music. I hope it doesn't start something, not that we're connected that tightly. Her family is small potatoes compared to us. But he is determined to go with her, bring back her things, and start a life with her. He wants to get married here, so I told him to get with Judith, our event coordinator, and figure it out. I'll give her a heads-up that he gets priority. He wants it soon." He sighed and scrubbed his face. "I may have to go to Ottawa to help."

"No problem. I can cover here."

He put his head back. "If I'd had any idea he'd pull this shit, I would have taken her to the galleries myself."

"No, you wouldn't," I scoffed. "You wouldn't begrudge him being happy."

"As long as she keeps making him happy."

"Roman," I said. "I saw how they looked at each other. Neither of them was faking it."

He smiled grimly. "I know."

"If there is trouble, we'll have his back."

He nodded. "Yes, we will." Then he smirked. "But the bastard is paying for the suite. He caused me a lot of shit, and he can afford it."

I laughed. "Noted."

CHAPTER 7
ALDO

I was tired later that evening. Between the drama with Luca and a busy day at the hotel and casino, I was ready to pack it in. But my stomach growled, and I needed to eat. I headed to Rolling Dice, walking in and scanning the place. For a moment, something in my chest tightened then relaxed as Vi came into view. She wore a new uniform today—red pedal pushers and a black-and-white polka-dot blouse that hugged her curves. The outfit showed off her legs and sexy cleavage to perfection. My pants suddenly felt a trifle tight, and I sat down before anyone noticed. Vi came over, frowning. "Don't you want to sit in the staff area?"

"No. It's quiet. No one will bother me."

She tilted her head, studying me. "You look tired."

"Long day."

"You want the usual?"

"Please."

I took out my phone, pretending to look at it, but covertly watching as she walked away.

Dammit, she was as sexy leaving as she was coming.

The thought of her coming another way filled my head. Her wrapped around my cock as I drove into her, her screams of pleasure filling the air.

I shook my head to clear it.

I needed to stop thinking that way. She was an employee. A woman looking for her life. She wouldn't be here long, and I had nothing to offer her to help her with her decision. I wasn't partner material. I was a one-time thing.

And somehow, I thought she deserved more than that.

I watched her bustling around. Taking orders, helping serve other sections. She was constantly busy. She was a pleasure to watch—graceful and elegant. Sexy. So fucking sexy. She had a scarf tied around her slender neck, jaunty and cute. She wore sneakers, the laces red and white, matching the scarf. I loved her attention to detail.

She brought over my Reuben and milkshake, sliding it in front of me.

"Salad?" I asked. "Where are my fries?"

"It would do you good to eat a salad," she informed me. "You need the vitamins."

Her concern warmed something inside me, but I didn't show her. "I'm in perfect health. I want fries."

"Eat your salad, and maybe you'll get some."

I picked up my sandwich, hiding my smile. No one else would dare speak to me that way. I liked it.

"I passed my trial period," she told me with a smile. "I was given two more uniforms, so I guess I'll be around for a while."

I wasn't surprised. Wanda had given her glowing reports.

"Good to know," I replied. "The uniforms work on you."

She grinned and winked. "I know," she replied, walking away with an exaggerated sway to her hips.

I liked it.

I liked her.

Far too much to be happy about it.

I ate, my phone mercifully silent. I surreptitiously stalked her around the deli, eating the damn salad and trying not to laugh when she brought me a small order of fries, informing me I had done well. She assured me I would thank her later. Her cheek and feistiness amused me. I was used to being treated with kid gloves. She didn't give a shit. It was refreshing.

I wanted to take her somewhere and thank her by showing her how healthy I was. The idea of using that jaunty little scarf to muffle her gasps of pleasure filtered through my head more than once. But I knew that wasn't a good idea.

I wiped my mouth, stiffening as I saw her lingering at another table where a man sat, alone. He had been there for a while, and more than once, I had noticed how his eyes followed her. How often she stopped by his table to check on him. The way his gaze lingered on her as she walked away.

I felt something angry and red drip into my chest at his obvious attraction. It bloomed and deepened when she brought him his tab, and he chatted at her, offering her his phone for her number. She shook her head, and he wrote something on a napkin and handed it to her, holding her hand longer than he should have as he pressed it to her palm. Fury began as she slipped it into the pocket of her apron. He left with a self-satisfied smile on his face. It took everything in me not to go after him and tell him she was off-limits.

I had no right to do that.

Instead, I followed her down the hall as she walked to the supply room, grabbing a stack of napkins. She turned, gasping when she saw me behind her.

"Aldo," she exclaimed, laying a hand over her heart. "I didn't hear you."

"Mr. Ricci," I retorted, my voice raspy and low with warning.

"*Mr. Ricci,*" she repeated, not at all worried.

"Too busy thinking about your admirer?" I asked, crossing my arms.

"What?"

"I saw him give you his number."

"Which I don't plan on using."

"Good," I snapped. "You can't date customers."

She lifted her chin. "Is this a new rule?"

"It's policy," I insisted.

"I'll have to ask HR about that." She began to move past me, but I shot my arm out, blocking her way. She stopped, lifting an eyebrow. "Excuse me."

I dipped my hand into her apron pocket, pulling out the napkin with the offensive number scrawled across it. "Ron," it read over the digits.

"No dating customers."

She turned, stepping nearer to me. I could feel her warmth. Smell the soft fragrance she wore. "Who should I date then, *Aldo*? Want to introduce me to someone? A friend, perhaps?"

"No," I snarled, my arm going around her waist and pulling her close. "No one."

"But I have needs," she whispered. "Who will help me with those?"

We were so close, our lips were almost touching. I felt her breath on my skin. Tasted her in the air. A low growl built in my chest. I yanked her closer, daring to cup her ass with my free hand. I almost groaned at the feeling of her. "Stop tempting me."

"I was only doing my job." She reached out, running her finger along my scruff. "I like this," she whispered. "I wonder how it would feel on my skin."

I covered her mouth with mine, kissing her in frustration. Her lips were soft and pliant. Full and welcoming. I kissed her harder, sliding my tongue in as her mouth parted. Her taste exploded in my head, filling my senses. I explored every part of her, running my tongue along her teeth, over the roof of her mouth, twining with hers. Groaning deep in my chest at the taste and feel of her. Wanting more. Needing more. Determined to have it. I cupped her ass fully, yanking her tight to me. She whimpered, lifting one leg and wrapping it around me. I settled between her thighs, my cock hard and aching for her. I ground against her, and she moaned, a low, throaty sound that ramped me up more.

And then I heard it. Footsteps and a voice calling her name.

Reality crashed down around me. We were in the supply closet of the restaurant. Wanda was looking for her.

I stepped back. Violet's eyes were wide, her lips wet. My cock screamed at being denied what he wanted.

I shook my head.

"I'm off in an hour," she whispered, pleading, reaching for me.

I shook my head.

"No."

And I left her.

VI

The bastard left. Like a coward. Heading in the opposite direction of Wanda and disappearing around the corner. The supply room door shut behind him, clicking into place quietly.

I bent and picked up the napkins, grabbing another package just as Wanda appeared, pushing open the door.

“Oh, there you are. Did the door stick again?” she asked.

“Um, yes. I was about to call and ask for help,” I improvised.

“I’ll get maintenance again.” She peered at me. “Are you all right? You’re a little sweaty.”

“I hate confined spaces,” I lied. I couldn’t tell my boss I had just had the hell kissed out of me by Aldo and if she hadn’t shown up, we’d be fucking like rabbits by now. Instead, I was turned on, angry, and shocked at his sudden withdrawal.

Frustrating man. I knew he was interested. I saw his glances. Felt his intensity. I saw the way he reacted to the customer giving me his number. He wasn’t the first customer to do so, and I doubted he’d be the last, but I was always polite. I never called them. I had no intention of doing so, but Aldo didn’t need to know that. Yet.

And after the stunt he’d just pulled, maybe I wouldn’t tell him.

I followed Wanda down the hall, silently planning my revenge.

ALDO

I was still kicking myself two days later over kissing Vi. If Wanda hadn't come looking for her, I would have lost my head and taken her right then and there. I was her boss, and fucking her in the supply room at the back of the restaurant was an HR issue waiting to explode.

But the taste of her lingered in my head. I swore I could still smell her. Feel her. Normally not one for kissing, I had a feeling I could kiss her endlessly and never tire of it. That smart mouth of hers was highly addictive.

I shook my head, recalling the way she had reached out when I pulled back. She had wanted me as much as I wanted her. But it was a recipe for disaster. I needed to avoid her.

Which meant no more visits to the Rolling Dice. No more walk-bys or check-ins.

It was odd how much that bothered me.

A knock at my door interrupted my thoughts. "In," I called.

One of the servers came in with a tray.

"I didn't order anything."

"It was ordered in person," he replied, sliding it onto my desk. "On your behalf."

He left, and I studied the tray. My favorite Reuben and fries. A vanilla milkshake, tempting, the condensation glistening on the glass. And an envelope with my name on it written in a feminine hand. I had no doubt who'd sent me dinner.

I took a bite of the sandwich, staring at the envelope, curious as to the contents. Would it be scathing? Angry? Was she upset?

I barked a laugh in the empty room. Of course she was upset. I should probably man up and apologize. Assure her it would never happen again.

I frowned as a thought occurred to me. She wasn't going to quit, was she?

My appetite gone, I set aside the sandwich and wiped my fingers. I tore open the well-sealed envelope and scanned the contents. I had to blink and reread it. Twice. Even then, I could barely believe what I held in my hands.

Pictures, printed onto a simple page of white paper.

Vi frowning at the camera.

I HAVE NEEDS.

Written under it.

Vi glaring.

YOU LEFT ME.

A picture of a shopping bag.

I TOOK CARE OF THEM.

A picture of the contents of the bag. A dildo.

A final picture of Vi smiling, lying back on a pillow.

MUCH BETTER.

I stared at the paper, unsure how to react. Then I began to laugh. The minx was trying to get me all riled. I had to admit the thought of her using the dildo ramped me up. Part of me wished she had sent me pictures of that, but I knew she was smart enough to know where to draw the line.

I sat back, rubbing my lips, letting my mind wander. I could imagine her on her sofa, those long legs spread, working the dildo between them, her free hand playing with the hard nipple of her breast. I wondered if she whimpered, moaned, or cried out. If she was loud or quiet in her gratification.

If she whispered my name as she came.

My cock swelled, hardened, thinking about it. Picturing her pleasuring herself, I stroked myself, shutting my eyes, imagining it was me between her open legs. My mouth on those hard nipples. My cock buried in her heat, possessing her. I stared at the pictures of her. Angry, smiling—either way, she was sexy. I wanted her.

She had taken a huge risk sending me this. I could call her to my office and fire her. Ream her out for crossing the line. Except, I'd done it first, kissing her and walking away. This was her payback, and I had to admit, it was good. So calling her in here to yell at her or fire her wasn't what I wanted to do.

I wanted to fuck her.

I was certain she knew, if given the options, which one I would choose.

I pushed back from my desk, knowing I had to take care of myself.

Then I had a purchase to make.

This game was on.

CHAPTER 8
VI

I was jumpy all night at work. I had no idea what had possessed me to send Aldo that note, but I was angry over him leaving me all juiced up and needy. Needy for him. On an impulse, I stopped at the adult store and bought the vibrating dildo, then snapped some pictures. It worked well but left me wholly unsatisfied—not that I would admit that to him. I wanted him to think he was nothing to me, since it seemed I was nothing to him.

I was almost disappointed when my shift ended and I didn't see him. I wasn't sure what I expected—for him to show up and drag me back to the supply room and finish what he started? Call me into his office and yell at me? Fuck me on his desk?

I'd take the former if I got the latter.

My only worry was that I had crossed a line and might lose my job. Except I had a feeling that wouldn't happen. I had seen the desire in his eyes. Saw the way his gaze lingered. Even Wanda had casually mentioned she noticed him checking in on the deli more often these days.

I hoped it was because of me.

I arrived home, tired. Weary from the suspense and slightly disappointed at his lack of response. That was one thing I hadn't counted on. I was certain he would react. I opened the door and went in, shedding my coat and dropping my sweater on the back of the sofa, stopping at the sight of the bag on the counter that separated the kitchen from the living space. It hadn't been there when I'd gone to work. I walked to the counter slowly, looking around. The room was empty. The door to my bathroom was open, and it, too, was vacant. You would have to be tiny to fit in my closet. It was the only storage, and it was full.

The bag was plain brown paper. No logo. Stapled shut. I sat down, pulling it open carefully and lifting out the box, my eyes widening as I took in the object.

It was another vibrator. Much more elaborate. Expensive.

Larger.

I read the note.

IF THAT SATISFIED YOU, WHAT I HAVE TO OFFER WILL RUIN YOU FOR ANYONE ELSE.

UNTIL THEN, THIS WILL HELP.

YOUR MOVE, SEXY GIRL.

A

I swallowed, then began to laugh. He was playing with me. Right along with me. How he'd gotten in, I had no idea. But I'd known it was him even before I'd opened the bag. I could smell him.

I took out the vibrator, studying it. It was certainly bigger than I was used to. And according to the note, not as generous as Aldo himself.

And he was basically telling me he'd prove it to me.

I needed to get him to deliver.

Soon.

I didn't respond to his gift right away. I decided to let him stew a little. Two nights later, I came out of the kitchen and spotted him in my section, staring intently in my direction. I delivered the meals I was carrying, grabbed the coffeepot, offering refills, topped up some water glasses, then made my way to his table. His gaze burned me up as I approached. I was wearing the polka-dot skirt and tight blouse. I had purposely undone an extra button when I was grabbing a fresh water pitcher, and I had hiked up the skirt a little. His eyes were dark and intense, the frown on his face making me want to dance with glee. There was no disguising the lust in his gaze or the way his hands gripped the edge of the table as if stopping himself from touching me.

I stopped, my notebook and pen poised. "Good evening, Mr. Ricci. The usual? Or would you prefer to hear the specials?"

He lowered his voice. "Are you on them?"

I laughed. "To the right customer."

For a moment, he didn't speak. He stared, undressing me with his eyes and fucking me in front of everyone. I felt the heat in my cheeks blossom and my limbs begin to tremble. He smiled slightly, knowing exactly how he was affecting me.

He leaned back, observing me. "Everything all right…at home, *piccola peste*?"

I smiled at him. I knew a little Italian and that I was being naughty. "Everything is great. I have a new friend. We are hanging out all the time. Just the two of us…such *good* times." I sighed. "Beyond good. Almost blissful."

His eyes narrowed. "I see."

"I should show you some pictures of our good times." I inched closer. "Unless, of course, you'd like to join us."

It was his turn to react. He sucked in a deep breath. I could feel all the rage and lust simmering below his cool exterior. God, I hoped I was close when it blew. I had a feeling I would never be the same.

"Careful what you wish for." He stood, stepping close, our bodies almost touching. "I've changed my mind. I'm no longer hungry. I'll be going."

He gripped my shoulders, sliding past me. I felt him. All of him. Hard behind the hidden folds of his jacket. I put out my hand to stop him. "I could make you hungry."

He stopped. "Oh, baby," he murmured, somehow looking as if he were discussing the weather—cool and unaffected. "I'm starved. Ravenous. I could eat for hours and not get my fill. But another time. When we are both—free."

The pulse between my legs kicked into high gear. My breathing picked up at his words and the meaning behind them. "Sunday," I whispered. "I'm off Sunday and Monday."

He smiled. "Good to know."

"I have a cell phone."

He lifted an eyebrow. "I see."

I rattled off the number. "In case, you know, you have a personal one and want to call me or anything."

He paused, nodded, and left. Five minutes later, I got a text from an unknown number, which I knew had to be his.

Show me

Was all it said.

I swallowed.

Time to up the ante.

ALDO

I stared at the screen, my gaze greedy. *Jesus*—she'd sent me a picture of herself, mid-orgasm. I was certain of it. Her mouth was open, her head flung back, one hand gripping her hair. Sweat beaded her forehead.

She was fucking perfection.

And I needed my hands on her.

Since she'd given me her cell number, the dirty texts, the hidden innuendos, and the occasional pictures had been traded. I walked a fine line, barely hanging on to my control. Saying and doing things I shouldn't be doing with an employee. Watching her from a distance, because if I got close, I wouldn't be able to keep my hands off her. She invaded my thoughts frequently and starred in my dreams. I woke up every day hard and aching, and nothing I did satisfied me.

My cock wasn't happy with my hand. It had no interest in another woman. It—*I*—wanted her.

"Aldo?"

I blinked, startled, looking over at Roman. "Sorry. What was that?"

He frowned. "If you glare at that screen any harder, it will implode. Problem?"

"Oh." I slid my phone into my pocket. "Nothing I can't handle."

I planned on handling it tonight.

"I'm heading to the estate in the morning. I'll be back Monday. You want to come for lunch?"

"No, I have things I need to take care of."

He looked puzzled. "Are you sure you're all right?"

"Yes."

"Okay. You with me tonight?"

"Until about two. I, ah, have a date."

He grinned. "Well, that is news. Anyone I know?"

I shrugged. "Doubtful."

He let it go. We didn't pry into each other's personal lives.

"We're letting the floor managers handle tomorrow, right?"

I nodded. "Sal and Raymond are covering. I'll be close if something comes up."

"I hope it doesn't. We both need a break from this place."

"How did Nonna take to Justine?"

"Loved her. I spoke with Luca earlier. Her family was surprisingly accepting. Her father was displeased, but Luca calmed him down. Her mother loved him, as did the rest of the females in the family."

I chuckled. "He is a charmer."

"They'll be married again here in short order. Judith is arranging the wedding and dinner. Luca and Justine want intimate. I'm sending them on a honeymoon." He raked a hand through his hair. "I'll step in and run things while he is gone. I'll need you here."

I nodded. "No problem."

He sighed, looking out the window. "Hopefully all goes well when he is away. His crew can handle most of it. He runs a tight ship. I'll just be the figurehead while he's gone."

"I'll cover here, Roman."

"I know." He stood, going to the door. "Enjoy your, ah, *date*. Is dinner involved or just dessert?"

I laughed. I wasn't known for dating. Neither of us was.

"Time will tell."

He lifted an eyebrow. "Well, she must be special if you're waiting to decide."

I waved him off.

He left, and my phone was out of my pocket before the door clicked shut. I stared at the photo again and went downstairs, speaking to Maurice directly. As usual, he was efficient, asking no questions, simply handing me what I required.

Back in my office, I sent a message.

> Room 1710 after work.
>
> Bring your friends.

Then I resolutely put everything out of my mind and did my job.

CHAPTER 9
VI

I stared at Aldo's text. As usual, it was short, precise, and caused millions of butterflies to flutter in my stomach.

My picture had accomplished what I wanted.

At least, I was pretty certain it had.

The past few days, I had been on tenterhooks. I never knew when a text would appear from him. What it would say. Except it was always provocative. And sometimes sweet.

You look fucking sexy in that uniform.

Another picture, Vi? Naughty girls get what they deserve.

Do you deserve my cock?

Take your break, you look tired.

That isn't a request.

I didn't see him, but I felt him. His presence. His gaze. Yet when I would look, he wasn't there, but I knew he had been.

And now, he wanted me to meet him upstairs.

I stood. I needed to get ready.

Hours later, I was a bundle of nerves. I had exfoliated, shaved, trimmed, and scrubbed. Washed my hair and blew it dry. Packed my "friends" and a change of clothes into my knapsack. At work, I could barely concentrate. My hands shook at times. I dropped a plate—a first for me. Even Wanda was concerned.

"You all right, dear? You're flushed."

"Um, bit of a headache."

She tutted. "Take a break. We're not overly busy."

I sat at the back with a milkshake, too tense to eat. At one, she approached me. "You take off. We're quiet, and I know you want Derek to have the hours."

I nodded, grateful. Derek's pregnant wife had been laid off, and they were scrambling. Wanda caught me trying to sneak some of my tip money into his jar, and since then, she had donated some every night we worked together on my behalf. I made way more than he did in tips, and I wanted to help. But I knew he would refuse my offer.

I headed to the staff room on the floor below, wondering about using the shower there to freshen up. I had over an hour before Aldo expected me. But when I opened my locker, I found an envelope inside, a passkey the only item in it. Nothing was written on it, but I knew it was for the room. I didn't even wonder how he'd gotten into my locker. They supplied the locks, so no doubt, he had a master. I thought about it for a moment and decided to head up and use the shower there. I would be waiting when Aldo arrived.

I stepped into the suite, gazing around. A huge bed occupied the space, with a sofa and a chair by the window overlooking the Falls. There was a small bar and kitchen area. It was luxurious and spacious, decorated in the same water-colored theme as the rest of the hotel. The ceilings were high, crown molding setting off the pattern in the stucco.

The bathroom was enormous, with a Jacuzzi tub and a multiheaded shower. I shut the door and slipped off my uniform, stepping in and soaping up quickly. I hoped I would have more time to enjoy the shower and maybe the tub later.

Unless he planned on fucking me and kicking me out right away.

When I was done, I brushed my teeth and slipped on the soft terry robe hanging on the back of the door. It was warm and large, but I appreciated the coverage.

For some reason, I was nervous. I couldn't recall a man making me nervous before Aldo. But he did something to my equilibrium.

I opened the door and stepped into the room, freezing. Leaning on the back of the sofa was Aldo. His suit jacket was folded over the top of the cushions, his tie lying on top. He had undone some buttons on his shirt and rolled up the sleeves, exposing his taut forearms. He held a glass of amber liquid, taking a sip as he stared at me, his expression intense. Dark. Glittering with purpose. His hair was damp, as if he, too, had just showered.

"You were early," he observed. "I saw you come up."

"I-I wanted a shower. Wanda let me go, and I thought…" I trailed off, unsure how to explain.

"Eager, baby?"

I lifted my head, pushing back my shoulders. "Anxious."

"This is only for tonight," he said.

"I know. We'll get it out of our system." I had already figured out Aldo didn't do long-term. Or relationships. I wasn't sure I would be satisfied with one night, but if it was all I could get, I would take it. I wanted him. "I'm a big girl, Aldo. I know how it is."

Something passed over his face, and he set aside his glass, holding out his hand. "Come here."

I crossed the room, taking his proffered hand. It was bigger than mine, the fingers long, the tips slightly callused. His skin was warm, and he tugged me closer.

"I want you," I murmured. "You're all I can think about."

"Me too, baby. Me too."

Our gazes locked, the passion flaring. I expected him to rip off the robe I was wearing and throw me over the sofa or on the bed and ravish me. Instead, he cupped my face between his warm palms, pressing his lips to mine. He kissed me slowly, thoroughly, sweetly. His tongue glided with mine in long, languid passes. He hooked an arm around my waist, drawing me closer so I was between his legs. I wrapped my arms around his neck, sinking into him. Into his kiss. I had never experienced a kiss like it. Powerful. Tender. Claiming.

I whimpered as he deepened the kiss, holding me tighter. I felt his erection pressed between us, and I dropped my hand, stroking him through the material of his pants. He groaned, spearing his hand into my hair and pulling—not hurting but, instead, caressing. We kissed endlessly. Hard and fast. Soft and sweet. Deep and carnal. We shared oxygen, neither of us wanting to separate our lips. We kissed until I was dizzy. Panting. Needy.

For him.

He dragged his lips along my cheek to my ear, and his voice was low, raspy, and sexy. "I want to see you, Violet. Show me what I've been waiting for."

I stepped back, slowly untying the belt and letting the folds of the robe fall open. He narrowed his eyes, his hands fisting the fabric of the sofa. I rolled my shoulders, letting the robe fall away. I stood in front of him naked, my shoulders back, my eyes locked on his. I didn't move as he swept his gaze over me. Once. Twice. Again. His gaze turned even darker, and he licked his lips. I felt his glance like a physical touch. Scorching and hot. I burned under his gaze. His pants tented obscenely, and he made no attempt to hide the fact.

"Violet," he murmured, his voice low and husky. He waited until I met his gaze.

"You are a goddess."

His words surprised me. Everything so far had surprised me. I wanted to surprise him.

I stepped closer and fell to my knees. "This goddess wants to worship you."

He sucked in a fast breath. "Jesus. Yes."

ALDO

Violet was all creamy skin and long legs. Her beautiful breasts were full and heavy, with dark rose-colored nipples that hardened as I stared at her. Her waist rounded out to wide hips I wanted to hold as I sank deep inside her. Everywhere I looked, I wanted to touch. To kiss. I needed to know how she tasted at the juncture of her neck. Behind her ear. If she whimpered or gasped as I sucked her nipples. How sweet and musky she would be when my tongue was in that sweet cleft between her legs. How she would look when I made her come. I wanted to watch her when I used my fingers, my tongue, and my cock to make her cry out.

When she sank in front of me, her words almost made me come right there. She never broke our gaze as she undid my belt and zipper, letting my pants drop to the floor before she slowly wrapped her hand around my already weeping cock.

"You call me naughty," she whispered. "Walking around naked under your suit."

"Only for tonight. For you."

My head fell back as she responded the very best way —by taking my cock in her mouth. I groaned as she lapped at the tip and tongued her way up and down my shaft. The world outside her mouth ceased to exist as she played with me, sucking and stroking, taking in as much of me as she could, using her hands on the rest. Cupping my balls, teasing me with her talented tongue. Humming around me so I felt the sensations everywhere. I grasped the back of her head, praising her, guiding her. She pushed at the material of my shirt, and I yanked it over my head, throwing it behind me somewhere. I didn't care where it landed. She traced the muscles of my abdomen, feathering her fingers along the ridges. Stretching her arms up to reach my nipples and flick them, all while sucking me. Then she stroked along my sides, reaching behind to cup my ass, pushing my cock farther down her throat.

I groaned and hissed. Watched her, watching me. Fought off the orgasm bearing down on me. But it was too strong, and she was far too good at this.

"Coming," I warned, giving her the chance to move. She shut her eyes and relaxed her throat, sliding her finger between my ass cheeks and teasing me.

I came hard. Loudly. Flooding her throat and cursing. Groaning her name. Pleading to God and any other deity that was listening. I gripped the back of the sofa as I let my release wash over me. Bright, powerful, intense. I wasn't sure I had ever felt one as strong. It went on and on, and I was certain my head was about to explode from the pleasure.

And then it receded, slowly ebbing until I was almost mindless.

I opened my eyes and gazed down at the beautiful woman between my legs. She smiled at me, then winked. "I was taking the edge off for you."

I pulled her to her feet and kissed her, tasting the sharpness of my release on her tongue.

"Your turn."

She grinned. "Bring it on, big man."

"On the bed," I growled, kicking off my shoes and stepping from my clothing. I yanked off my socks, my erection already growing again as I watched her back up to the bed and sit.

"Lie back."

She did as I demanded, sliding toward the middle, keeping her legs closed and smiling at me, looking too damn sexy and coquettish. I approached the bed and slid my hands down her shapely thighs. I lifted a leg, kissing the delicate bones of her ankle. Her foot was slender and long, the arch high and her toes painted a deep pink. "Such amazing legs." I kissed the arch. "A dancer's legs and feet."

She laughed. "You mean waitress."

"You make every step look like you're dancing."

Her eyes softened. "You say the nicest things for a tough guy."

"Only for you," I repeated.

I kissed her other ankle and ran my hands up her legs, gripping her knees. "But while you're here, in this room, baby, the legs stay open." I pushed at her knees, exposing her to my eyes. Deep pink, wet, and glistening. Her pussy had a small thatch of curls and was pretty. Beckoning. Begging for me.

So I gave it what it wanted.

She gasped as I covered her with my mouth, lapping at her clit and tasting her. She gripped the comforter, her back arching. She was musk and honey. Sweet and sharp. Wet and warm. I couldn't get enough. I licked and bit, sucked and nuzzled. Slid one finger, then two into her, pumping in a steady rhythm until she climaxed, crying out my name. But I wasn't done. Not by a long shot. I sat back.

"On your knees," I ordered, rolling on a condom.

She did as I asked, looking over her shoulder at me as she propped herself up on her elbows. She had a tattoo that snaked up her spine of a flock of swallows taking off in flight. The black ink was sexy on her long back. She was flushed and eager, wiggling her ass. I smacked it once, then twice, her skin turning pink. "You want my cock, baby?"

"Yes. Now."

I laughed, smacking her butt again. "I call the shots here."

But I gripped her hips and sank in deep, groaning at how good she felt around me. I reached under her, cupping her heavy breasts, playing with her nipples as I began to move. She whimpered, matching my movements, and we flowed together like a tidal wave, surging and ebbing, hard and fast. She whimpered and moaned.

"You feel so good. There. Oh God, yes. *Right there.*"

She lifted her ass higher.

"More, Aldo. Give me more."

I sat back, taking her with me, sinking even deeper as I pulled her to my chest, cinching an arm around her waist and holding her close. She cried out at the angle, reaching up and gripping my neck, lifting her head, her mouth searching for mine. I kissed her hard, mimicking my actions with my tongue, mouth-fucking her. I slid my hand down, rubbing hard, fast circles on her clit. She gasped into my mouth and tightened around me. It set off my orgasm, the pleasure racing through me, her walls gripping and fluttering. I dropped my head to her shoulder, moaning her name, my cock pulsating, my orgasm continuing far longer than I had ever experienced before. Something about this woman did that to me. I couldn't get enough.

Slowly we came down from the high we were on, the sensations lessening. She still gripped me inside her, the occasional flutter making me groan. I lifted her off me, carefully laying her on the bed. I disposed of the condom and returned to her. She lay on her side, looking thoroughly fucked and pleasured. Without a thought, I climbed in beside her, pulling her into my arms. She fit there as if made for me, her softness forming a perfect shadow to my harder body.

"Do you want me to go?"

"I'm far from finished with you," I replied.

"Good," she mumbled, her voice sleepy.

In a gesture I didn't recognize, I pressed a kiss to her forehead. "Sleep a bit, baby. I need you rested for round two."

"Mmm," she murmured. "Looking forward to it."

And she was out.

I gazed down at her in the low light. She was truly lovely. Her milky skin was set off by the darkness of her hair. Long lashes fluttered on her cheeks as she slumbered. Her skin was like silk under my fingers. In the quiet deep of the night, I could admit to myself she was as perfect a match for me as I had ever met.

Strong, stubborn, funny. Sexy and independent, yet I sensed a vulnerability she hid from the world.

But I wasn't looking for anything permanent. She knew that and accepted it. She said the same thing.

I shut my eyes, deciding to relax a bit before waking her up for more.

I refused to listen to that low voice in my head that wondered if maybe what we weren't looking for had found us anyway.

CHAPTER 10
VI

"More," I groaned as the sensations flowed through me, lighting my nerves on fire. "Give me more, big man."

Aldo chuckled, the sound deep and dark in the room. I was on my knees again, all of me on display for his eyes. The smaller of my two dildos was in my ass, the larger one inside my pussy. He was watching as he fucked me with them, whispering dirty words, telling me how sexy I looked as he pumped both toys into me.

"What more can I give you?" he asked.

"Your cock. I want you," I replied.

In seconds, the dildo was gone and his much-larger cock filled me. He lifted me higher, the steady hum of the dildo and his powerful thrusts sending me skyrocketing. I felt my orgasm in every part of my body—even my fingers and toes pulsated. I cried out his name, screaming into the fluffy pillow as he moved, shifting and lifting a leg to add even more power behind his movements. My body spasmed, and I whimpered as I felt yet another orgasm building. How he did that, I had no idea, but I wasn't certain I would survive yet another one.

"Aldo, please," I begged. "I can't."

"Oh baby, you can. You will. And later, you'll thank me by sucking me off again." He reached under me, sliding his fingers over my engorged clit and playing with it. "I want to hear you this time. Give it to me."

I was caught in a wave of pleasure. Intense, mind-blowing, incredible hedonism I had never experienced. Aldo was relentless. He had been all night. Every time I thought we were done, he started again. His mouth, his fingers, the dildos, his cock.

I wasn't going to be able to move.

But the orgasms, the feeling of his hard, strong body over mine, under it, behind me, was too much to resist. I couldn't say no.

I didn't want to.

My orgasm hit me unexpectedly. Hard. Fast. Wild. I cried out, his name falling from my lips, my body quaking and shivering, my pussy clamping down on him. He groaned my name, thrusting until his own release happened.

Then we slowed, stopped, and collapsed.

He pulled me into his arms, and I went happily, surprised to discover earlier that Mr. One Night Only was a snuggler. He held me close, pressing kisses to my head and cradling me against his body.

"You are incredible," he whispered quietly.

"We are incredible together," I replied.

For a moment, he was quiet.

"Yeah, we are," he said. I felt his lips on my head. "Thanks, baby," he murmured.

I could only hum in acknowledgment, sleep claiming me.

I patted his arm. "Stay."

I was out before he could reply.

I woke up to the morning light diffusing through the room. The curtains were open, the view of the Falls spectacular. I sat up, my body protesting. He'd been all over me all night, and I had lost count of the number of orgasms I'd had and the various ways he'd used my body.

All of it had been incredible. But he had stated clearly it was only for the night.

I was alone, Aldo's side of the bed empty and cold. Disappointment tore through me, although I wasn't surprised. I had hoped he'd have breakfast with me at least. I stood slowly, letting my body adjust. The robe I had used the night before was on the foot of the bed, and I slid it on and headed to the bathroom. After I was done, I wandered back to the room. It was only ten, so I had an hour to check out. I sat on the chair, staring out of the window. I rarely got to see the Falls this way. They were mesmerizing.

The door opening made me look up. Aldo walked in, dressed in another suit, looking fresh and handsome in that rugged way of his.

He pulled a cart in behind him and frowned when he saw me.

"I thought you'd still be asleep."

"I thought you'd gone."

"I had to handle a couple of things. Then I got dressed in my suite and brought breakfast. I was letting you sleep."

My heart warmed at his words. He hadn't simply left.

"Oh."

"Hungry?"

I grinned. "Starved."

"I assumed so." He stopped by my chair, surprising me when he bent and kissed me. "You expended a lot of energy last night."

"We both did."

He kissed me again. "I know."

He took off his jacket, sitting down and rolling up his sleeves. I watched him covertly, but he caught me, lifting an eyebrow. "What?"

"It's sexy when you do that."

"Do what?" he asked, picking up a croissant and taking a bite. His throat moved as he swallowed.

"Roll up your sleeves. I love the way your muscles flex." I paused. "You're sexy when you eat too."

He froze, the croissant partway to his mouth. His eyes darkened. "You were pretty damn sexy last night as I ate you," he said, his voice low and gravelly.

My core clenched at his words, and I shifted in my seat. I stared at him, running my tongue along my bottom lip, his words lighting me up.

"Stop," he said. "You have to be sore."

"The night is over," I reminded him.

"And a new day has started." He reached over and poured us coffee. "Maybe we should talk about that."

I took the cup from his hand, our fingers brushing, our eyes locking. I felt a flutter in my stomach at his touch.

"Maybe we should."

He nodded. "Eat first. You're going to need it."

I didn't leave the hotel room that day. In fact, I didn't leave until it was time for my shift the following night. Aldo dropped by the room frequently. We had sex sometimes. Others, he sat and talked to me. We ate dinner together. He even got into the bath with me, although I had to promise him a blow job to do so. Once I made the offer, he couldn't get out of his suit fast enough, which made me laugh. He pretended to get angry and grabbed me, kissing me hard, and I slipped down into the water, taking him with me. Bubbles and water went everywhere, and he looked askance at the mess, then decided it didn't matter when I wrapped my hand around his hard cock and stroked him. He sat on the edge of the large tub as I sucked him, watching me the whole time, groaning and encouraging me. After I was done, he did the same for me, and I saw why he was so fascinated. The floor-to-ceiling mirror on the other end of the tub reflected his strong back muscles as he surged forward. My legs over his shoulders and the way his back moved were hypnotic. Looking down to see his face buried between my legs was erotic. His eyes were on me, and our gazes were as hot as the space around us. The steam-filled room was full of our noises. The sounds of the water splashing, the mist gathering on the edges of the mirror, his large hands clamped around my thighs. All of it was sexy, intimate, and raw.

I headed down to my shift, trying not to feel sad as I shut the door behind me. My two days of Aldo were over. When he'd left earlier, he had kissed me the same way he had when I'd come out of the shower, my face trapped between his hands, his caress tender, his goodbye unspoken. I had smiled at him, refusing to allow him to see my distress. I had thought once we were together, that intense pull I felt toward him would stop.

It had, in fact, gotten stronger.

But I knew the rules. Aldo had already bent them, giving me extra time. He hadn't said anything about seeing me again, simply telling me to hang in the suite as long as I wanted before heading to work. When he left, I stared at the door, my heart aching a little. I had a feeling falling for him would be easy. Natural. Like breathing.

But he had made it clear, he wasn't interested in anything beyond this room.

And I had told him I was a big girl and could handle it. And that was exactly what I intended to do.

I finished my shift and headed to my car. I hadn't eaten much, my appetite off. My apartment looked blah and dreary after the luxury of the hotel room. The bathroom seemed even smaller than before, and I already missed that large tub. I showered and sat on the sofa, a glass of water in my hand. I decided on my next day off I would go buy a bed. The sofa was going to feel cramped and lonely tonight. I was already dreading it.

I shook my head in exasperation. I had only slept beside him for two nights. Less, if I counted the times he would slip from the bed, dress, and head down to solve a problem. But I knew he was coming back. And I also knew, when he did, he would wake me with his mouth on my skin and take me again.

I shivered thinking about it. Recalling how it felt being with him. His possession and the way he used my body. The pleasure he took and gave. The unexpected tenderness he showed. His thoughtful gestures. His insistence there was no room in his life for a relationship, yet when we were together, that was how he acted.

As if we were together.

He fussed. Worried. Cared. Took. Gave. Then he walked out.

He was an enigma.

I shut my eyes and curled up on the sofa.

I wished he were my enigma.

I was dragging my feet by the time my shift ended the next night. I had barely slept, and the deli was busy all evening. I didn't even get a break. I opened my locker, stopping at the sight of the small envelope waiting for me.

> 2301.
>
> Come to me.

The short directive was written in Aldo's bold, dark script. I picked up the envelope and opened it. It contained the passcard needed to get to that floor and let me into the room. I leaned my head on the metal door, knowing I had two choices. Go upstairs and let him fuck me, or head home and end this. I knew if I didn't show up, he wouldn't reach out again. If I was honest, I wanted to feel him again, but I didn't want to be his booty call.

And I was so tired.

I decided I had a third choice. I could go up and tell him. Be honest. Surely he would understand I was too exhausted to play tonight.

I was nervous heading up in the elevator, grateful to be the only occupant. I hesitated at the door, then swiped the card and walked in. Aldo wasn't there, the room empty. I looked around, curious. The room was even more decadent than the suite we'd been in before. And it felt different—almost personal. I inhaled, realizing I could smell Aldo. His scent hung in the air, saturating the room. Not as if he'd just walked through it, but as if he were part of the room. I set down my bag and looked around. This wasn't a random room he'd procured for the night. This was his personal suite. Some of his suits hung in the closet. A damp towel was flung over the bathroom door, and his toiletries were in the drawers. There were a few casual clothes in the dresser. A deep black robe was tossed over the back of a chair, and I realized it matched the chair in my apartment—only larger. The small bar area held coffee pods, and unable to resist, I opened the small fridge. It was filled with water and a bag of apples.

I blinked as I looked around. He'd brought me to his private place.

Why?

The door opened, and he strode in, stopping when he saw me. For a moment, neither of us said a word. Then he crossed the room, cupping my face and pulling me into a hard, deep kiss.

"I wasn't sure you'd come."

"I can't stay."

"Why?" he demanded, his grip on my face tightening.

"I'm exhausted, Aldo. I barely slept last night—I don't have what you need tonight."

He pressed his forehead to mine. "All I need is you. Here. With me. I saw you at the deli and noticed how tired you looked. I just want to sleep next to you tonight. I barely shut my eyes without you."

I looked at him, seeing the tiredness etched on his skin. His gaze was dark and intense. Filled with something I didn't expect. Didn't understand.

Need.

"What's happening?" I asked quietly.

"I have no idea, but I'm not fighting it. Stay. Please," he added.

I knew that wasn't a word he used a lot.

"Yes."

CHAPTER 11
ALDO

I hadn't been able to get her out of my mind since I had left her in the suite. Memories of the hours we'd spent together played on rewind in my head. How well suited we were. How incredible we were together. She was beyond sexy, and I loved being inside her. Having her talented mouth on me. Everywhere. I liked everything about her. Her laughter, teasing. Her intelligence and how easy it was to talk to her. She'd asked me questions, and I had answered honestly. I had told her about my parents and growing up with Roman, omitting a lot of details, but still sharing.

"Is he, ah, mafia?" she asked quietly. "Are you?"

I met her gaze, her hazel eyes a soft blue in the low light of the room. "We're dangerous," was how I replied. "Powerful. Roman, especially."

"You protect him."

"And I will until I die."

"Would you die for him?"

"Without a thought."

She pressed herself to me. "Then be extra careful, Aldo. I like you in one piece with your heart beating."

The urge to tell her my heart hadn't really beat until she came into my life was strong, but I resisted.

"My heart or my cock?" I teased.

She slid her hand between us, touching my chest, then wrapping it around my thickening erection. "Both."

I had observed her leave last night, standing unseen in the shadows as she got in her old car and drove away. It took all my willpower not to stop her. I worked until the early morning hours, Roman prowling by my side. Our managers often handled everything, but Roman liked to make an appearance, never maintaining a consistent schedule. It kept everyone on their toes.

Tonight, I had seen Vi arrive, looking weary. As weary as I felt. I stayed clear of the deli but studied her via the security feed. She was quieter than normal, not as animated with the customers. It bothered me knowing she was tired. I frowned as I stared at the screen, wondering when Vi had become someone I worried over.

Roman had interrupted me, his voice over my shoulder. "What are you staring at so intently?"

"Just looking."

"You've been staring at the feed for ten solid minutes." He narrowed his gaze. "At the woman. Violet."

I stayed quiet.

He lifted his eyebrows. "Was she the date? The one you kept the room for?"

I shut down the feed, shuffling some papers. "Maybe."

"Are you hitting that? She must be a good lay if you got a room for her."

"Hey," I snapped. "Show a little respect."

Roman looked startled. "Aldo," he said. "What is going on?"

"Nothing." I scrubbed my face.

"Something, I think."

I shook my head. "Damned if I know."

He muttered something about the water and sat down at his desk. "First Luca, now you."

"It's not like that."

He chuckled. "I'll remind you of that someday."

I chose to ignore him.

Later, I was crossing the floor when I saw her again. She was outside the deli, leaning against the wall. Not doing anything but standing there. Her hands were behind her back, and she looked at the floor, her shoulders bent. She seemed to be staring at her feet. Then she rolled her shoulders, shook her head, and wiped under her eyes. Something pulled at my chest. Was she crying? Why was she crying? I felt my hands curl into fists, and I wanted to rush across the lobby, storm the deli, and find out why she was upset.

But I couldn't. If there was a problem, Wanda would deal with it. If I raged in and caused a scene, Vi would be furious. She was strong. Independent. Those were two of the many traits I found so attractive about her.

Instead, I went to the front desk and got a passcard for my room. My personal room.

And now here we were.

She was beyond exhausted. I could see the weariness etched on her skin. The dullness of her eyes. That she agreed to stay pleased me. I held out my hand.

"I'll fill the tub. We can relax, then sleep. I'll get you food if you're hungry."

"I'm just tired. You'll stay?"

"Yes." Roman had looked shocked when I'd informed him I was gone for the night, but he simply nodded and said he'd handle it.

She slipped her hand into mine, and I pulled her to me. She came willingly, resting her head on my shoulder, her body aligned with mine perfectly. She was the perfect height for me, I decided.

I pressed a kiss to her head. "Let me take care of you tonight. Just tonight, baby."

She hummed in agreement. "I'd like that."

"Then let me."

She sighed, leaning heavily into me. "Okay."

VI

I woke the next morning, surprised to find Aldo there. He was sitting in the chair, the robe wrapped around him, a book open on his lap. A steaming cup of coffee was sitting on the table beside him, and he had his ankle crossed over his knee. His feet were bare. He had long toes and surprisingly elegant feet for a man his size, and like the rest of him, they were looked after.

"Do you get pedicures?" I asked, sitting up against the headboard.

He looked up, startled. His eyes were set off by a pair of heavy tortoiseshell frames. He tugged them off, offering me a bashful grin. "Yeah. I'm on my feet a lot. They do a great pedi downstairs. I'm a regular." He set aside his book and picked up his coffee. "I can arrange one for you."

"That would be nice, thanks."

He smiled. "I like that."

"Like what?"

"That I offer you something and you don't simper and pretend you don't want it. It pleases me to give you things and you accept them gracefully."

"I have a feeling a pedicure won't break you, but it is a luxury for me."

"I'll arrange it." He studied me. "You look better. Do you need to cut back your hours? Change to day shift?"

I pulled my knees to my chest. "I need not to be ravished all night and day long for forty-eight hours."

He nodded, stroking his thumb along his bottom lip. "We'll space it out better. Fucking and sleeping." He paused, looking uncertain—something I didn't expect from Aldo. "If you're, ah, interested."

"You want honesty?" I asked.

"Always."

I rested my chin on my knees and took in a deep breath. "Aldo, I didn't sleep after I was with you. I felt like I was missing something. The thought of our time being over made me sadder than losing my entire life and home a few weeks ago. I like you. I like being with you." I swallowed. "Even if it's not forever."

He studied me quietly. "I haven't taken a full night off in months. Maybe longer. It took all my strength to leave you this morning and do some rounds. I rushed around, desperate to get back before you woke up. Watching you sleep calms me. Knowing I'm watching over you, that you're safe, makes me feel…" He trailed off. "It makes me feel something."

"I do feel safe with you."

"I trust you," he informed me. "I have never once had a woman come to my room here."

"Usually a different one every night?" I teased, even though I hated the thought of him with another woman.

"Usually a different hotel and a few hours—if that. And it was a rare occurrence. I'm not a player," he replied. "I have never spent this much time with another person, aside from Roman."

"Does he know?"

"He knows some, not all. I can't explain it to him, when I can't understand it myself."

I smiled.

"But I don't want to talk about it yet, until I figure it out. With him or with you. Can you handle that? I want you with me when you can be. When I can be here. I want to spend more time with you."

"I'd like that."

He looked pleased. Our eyes locked, the heat and desire between us sizzling.

"You know what I'd like even more?" I whispered.

He stood, shrugging off his robe. It dropped to the floor in a pool of ebony, and he stood gloriously naked, his erection growing, his muscles taut and his gaze intense. "Hopefully, what I want as well," he said.

"Well, I meant coffee. But if your dick is on the menu, I could eat," I replied, quirking my eyebrows.

He chuckled and came closer. "How about both, baby? My dick first, and I'll get you coffee and anything else you want after."

I swung my legs off the bed, and I took him in my hand, stroking his cock, loving how he groaned. I opened my mouth, sliding him in, swirling my tongue on the head.

"Yeah, baby, like that," he praised. "Such a gifted mouth. Such a pretty, talented girl I have."

I slid my hands to his ass, cupping the firm cheeks, taking him deeper. He groaned, delving his fingers into my hair. "Vi," he murmured. "Jesus. *Yes. Suck me. Hard.*"

I did as he asked.

I was really hoping for pancakes.

The next while passed in a blur of days and nights. Sometimes I couldn't tell them apart. But every day, Aldo was part of my world. Sometimes a visit at the deli, a few moments shared over a sandwich, some random texts or a call. There were nights I spent in his suite. A few he stayed at mine. The single bed I'd bought and put under the window was better than the sofa but not by much. At least he could almost fit. I didn't have room for a king-size bed to accommodate him. We snuggled a lot on those nights, although he was certainly inventive when it came to sex. I knew he had a real residence—a house—somewhere in town, but he never took me there, and I didn't ask. Our relationship had boundaries, and I was smart enough to know that. And as sad as it made me, I accepted them, because I loved being with him. I also knew our relationship was different from others he'd had in the past. I saw the way he watched me. His protectiveness and his possessive side. He hated it when customers were overly friendly, his gaze darkening, the furrow between his brows deepening. He was always more passionate later, as if claiming me.

What he didn't realize was that I was his. Completely. I had fallen for him without knowing. The day he walked away, I wasn't sure how I was going to handle it. I would have to leave Niagara Falls and everything behind. The thought of it saddened me. I no longer got excited when I stashed my tip money away. It wasn't a fund to do something thrilling or save for my future.

It was the fund I would need when I left Aldo and his world behind.

Because, despite his words, I was worried that day would come. I wasn't sure he would ever be comfortable enough to share his feelings. To completely open up to me. It bothered me, thinking of him alone for the rest of his life.

That made me sadder than anything else.

CHAPTER 12
VI

The deli was crazy tonight—even more so than normal. The weekends were always busy, but it had been particularly warm and people liked to be inside where it was cool. Still, the lingering heat outside made them cranky. I had more than the usual number of complainers tonight. And one man who was seated in my section had been a pain in my ass from the moment he'd sat down. His water wasn't cold enough. Then I added too much ice. The coffee was too strong. Then tepid. He stared at me incessantly, making me uncomfortable. There was something about his stare that creeped me out. The words thank you and please were not in his vocabulary. He was rude and condescending, barking at me constantly. Wanda had already spoken to him, but we agreed quietly between us he was one of those people who would never be happy. He'd been angry when he walked in, and he was looking for someone to take it out on.

I was the lucky one tonight. All I could do was smile and grit my teeth. He'd be gone soon enough, and I could forget him.

When I slid his burger and onion rings in front of him, he scowled.

"Is there a problem, sir?" I asked politely, adding "dickhead" in my head to the end of the sentence.

"I said extra onions."

"They added extra, and I will bring you more when I come back with your fries."

"You call this an order of rings? What are there—six? With the prices you charge, there should be more. What a rip-off joint." He jerked his thumb toward the casino. "Just like them, the fuckers."

"Let me fix that for you."

In the kitchen, I took a deep breath and counted to ten—twice. I got more grilled onions, another plate of rings, the fries, and poured him a fresh coffee. What he thought of this place didn't matter, and I knew better than to take it personally. But it pissed me off.

And the extras I brought to him didn't even make him happy. His snippets of complaints became louder.

“You spilled my coffee. What the hell kind of waitress are you?”

He had jostled my arm while I filled the cup. I got him a fresh one.

“This table is wobbly.”

He’d pushed it around so much, one of the feet had fallen off. I had a busboy help me put it back on. There was no way I was kneeling in front of that asshole.

“Who decorated this place? It looks like the fifties threw up in here.”

I resisted telling him his mother had.

“This burger tastes like shit. You’re serving crap.”

Other diners were looking at him, a few glaring. He was bothering everyone and I wanted to tell him to leave, but it wasn’t my place.

Wanda spoke with him again, even comping his meal, but it didn’t help. He became angrier and belligerent. “The fucking casino stacks the decks and fixes the machines so they take all your fucking money, and now they serve shit food too?”

“I’m sorry you’re dissatisfied. Is there anything I can do?” I asked, barely holding on to my temper.

He sat back. “You could get on your knees and suck my dick.”

I heard Wanda gasp, and I was done.

I leaned close. "I doubt I could find it without pepper and tweezers."

He narrowed his eyes and grabbed my arm, squeezing it tight. "What did you say, bitch?"

I tried to shake off his hold. "You heard me. You can leave now. Your meal is on the house. Don't worry about a tip."

He yanked me closer. "You wouldn't be getting one, you self-righteous little fuck. But I am going to give you something you won't forget."

I laughed. "I doubt that."

"I don't know who owns this shithole, but I have a thing or two I'd like to tell them."

A voice spoke up behind me. "Well then, today is your lucky day. I happen to own this *shithole*, as you call it, and I would be interested in hearing your thoughts on the matter. But first, get your hands off her."

"Right. Fucking. Now," Aldo's voice added, barely restrained fury deepening it.

The customer released my arm, and I stepped aside, relief flooding through me. Roman and Aldo stood behind me, looking like walking death. Both were serious. Intense. Threatening.

"I don't appreciate my staff being harassed, touched, or threatened. Nor do I like the tone, the language, or the insults you are throwing around. You're disturbing the other diners and upsetting everyone." Roman tugged his shirt sleeves down and rolled his neck. "This casino and everything associated with it, including the restaurants and my staff, are, without a doubt, impeccable. Even that simple burger you ate is made from the best ingredients we can purchase. So your criticism is more indicative of your shitty frame of mind than actual fact."

Aldo murmured something, and Roman lifted one eyebrow. "Perhaps the large sum of money you lost has made you forget your manners. I think you need to come with us and be reminded of how to use them."

"Fuck you, asshole," the man said, pushing out of the booth.

I watched the scene unfold in front of me. Everyone was watching. Roman laughed at his words, looking at Aldo. "Did you hear that? *Fuck you*, he said. As I stated, no manners."

"He called you an asshole, too," Aldo replied dryly. "Hardly imaginative."

"I'm leaving," the customer snarled.

Roman nodded. "Yes. You are. Permanently."

"What?"

"You are banned. Effective this moment. You are no longer welcome in my buildings. Here, or anywhere."

The customer's face darkened. He glowered, almost spitting in his rage. Then he acted like an idiot.

I gasped as he took a swing at Roman. To his credit, Roman didn't move—he didn't even blink or look shocked. In an instant, Aldo had the customer in a headlock, and a moment later, two other men appeared and dragged him from the restaurant, with him cursing and yelling the whole time. Then, like a faucet, the noise was shut off.

Roman looked around. "I'm sorry for your meals being interrupted. Everything is on the house. I hope what occurred tonight won't stop you from coming back."

The people in the restaurant clapped. Actually clapped.

Roman turned to me, his voice quiet. "Nothing like dinner and a show. Are you all right, Ms. Nelson?"

"Yes."

He glanced between me and Aldo, who was watching me with narrowed eyes. His shoulders were tense, and he looked as if he was about to explode.

"I'll leave you two to talk. Aldo, you know where I'll be."

Aldo nodded. Roman left, stopping to shake a few hands and speak to Wanda. Aldo looked at me. "My office. Now."

I could only follow.

ALDO

My blood was boiling with rage. Roman and I had come to the restaurant after Wanda called, worried about a brewing problem. I observed Vi trying to placate the customer to no avail. He became louder, angrier. She remained calm.

When he grabbed her, I was done.

"I will fucking end him," I growled and rushed into the restaurant, Roman hot on my heels.

I didn't know what Vi had said to him, but his face turned almost purple. Roman and I heard his last outburst, and I let Roman speak. He liked to deal with assholes and dish out their punishment. Part of me wanted to follow Roman and work this jerk over, but the bottom line was that I was more concerned with

Vi. The need to make sure she was all right was paramount.

And that took priority.

We didn't speak on the way to my office. I walked alongside her, my hand on the small of her back, and I refused to stop.

As soon as we were in my office, I shut the door and ran my hands down her arms, inspecting her. I could see the reddened marks where his fingers had dug into her skin, which only made me angrier.

"Are you all right?"

"I'm fine, Aldo. Really."

I lifted her arm closer to the light, inspecting the marks. They would be bruises by morning. "He was grabbing you. Hurting you."

She cupped my face. "And you stopped him. Thank you. He didn't get a chance to really hurt me. He was just being a complete asshole."

"What did he say that made you so mad as we got there?"

"He told me to suck his dick. I told him I couldn't find it unless I had pepper and tweezers, so good luck with that."

I looked at her, and she grinned. *Grinned.* She'd been verbally abused and attacked as far as I was concerned, and she was trying to make me smile.

Her hands tightened on my cheeks. "I'm fine, Aldo. Let it go."

She didn't know me at all if she thought I was letting this go. Or maybe she was asking, hoping I would.

"He will be banned from the hotel and the casino. He won't bother you again."

"Good. Now can I go back to work?"

I stared at her in wonder. "My room. Tonight."

She smiled. "Add in a bath with me, and I'll say yes."

I nodded. Before her, I had never had a bath as an adult. Showers were faster. But I did like to lie in the warm water with her, feeling her close to me. I pulled her into my embrace, needing the contact, not ready to let her go just yet.

"I'll get you more of those lavender salts you like," I offered.

"Perfect."

After I was calmer, I walked her back to the deli. Wanda told her she didn't have to finish her shift, and Vi simply laughed, shook her head, and got back to work. I headed to Roman's office, finding him freshly showered. He glanced at me as he poured some scotch, offering me a glass.

"Is she all right?"

"Shaken up, but she's strong. She's back at the deli. She insisted."

He looked impressed.

"Where is that piece of shit?"

"Gone."

"Permanently?"

He laughed dryly. "Too many people saw us together, Aldo. He isn't dead."

"Shame."

"He has a temper he can't control. He was almost frothing at the mouth when I went downstairs. He informed me if it was just the two of us, I'd be sorry."

I sat down with a grin. "So…"

He shrugged. "I told the boys to let him go. Gave him his chance."

"And?"

"Let's say he is going to be sore in the morning. Breathing in might be a problem."

"Did he get a hit in at all?"

"Only his head when I stepped aside and he hit the wall. Then he lunged again—sort of like a bull, snorting and angry. I took him out in two fast punches. Shame it happened so fast." He sipped his scotch. "The boys took pictures, he was informed he was no longer welcome, and they delivered him to his car. I comped his parking. After his losses at the tables, I'm not sure he had enough money left to pay for it, and since I confiscated his player pass, he had no way out other than that option."

I smirked as I took a sip.

"I had them put a tracker on his car. We'll put his face in the system, so if he comes back, we'll know."

"Good."

He watched me. "I decided to let him go before you showed up, Aldo. I wasn't sure he'd make it out the door."

"He grabbed her. Put marks on her."

"And this matters to you because…?" He paused. "And don't tell me it's because she's an employee."

I met his gaze. "I have been with her almost every night since our date."

His eyebrows shot up. “Still?”

“Yes.”

“Aldo. What are you saying?”

I shook my head. “I have no idea. But there is something between us. I can’t deny it.”

“Are you seeing her later?”

“She has a pass for my room. My private room.”

“Holy fuck,” he mumbled.

“She makes me feel different. Think different. I think I want—” I stopped. “I don’t want to talk about it.”

“I don’t either. Next thing you know, we’ll be braiding each other’s hair and sipping wine.”

I had to laugh. “God forbid.”

He finished his scotch and stood. “I’m going downstairs.” He paused at the door. “If you need time, if she needs anything, it’s yours, Aldo.”

“Thanks.”

He met my eyes. “You care about her. Then she’s important to you. Which makes her important to me.”

And he walked out.

CHAPTER 13
ALDO

I headed to the deli before Vi's shift was over, and I walked with her across the lobby and up to my room. She was quiet but calm. We had a bath, floating in the lavender-scented water. She loved the aroma of the soothing plant, and I knew I would never smell it again without thinking of her—of our time together.

As I contemplated the thought, another one occurred to me.

What if I asked her to stay? To be part of my life? Would she want that? We never discussed the future.

"What are your plans, Vi?"

"Tonight?" she hummed. "Hopefully your massive cock inside me, a few orgasms, and a good sleep."

I dropped a kiss to her head. "That is guaranteed. I mean later. A few months from now, a year…" I trailed off.

"Hmm," she hummed. "I don't know."

"Do you want to be a waitress your whole life?"

"No. Maybe go back to school. I always loved numbers and wanted to be an accountant."

"Then you should."

"When I'm ready."

"Some good schools around here. Niagara College has accounting courses."

She turned and looked up at me. Her skin glowed from the steam in the room, her hair pushed off her face. "Want to keep me around longer, big man?" she asked, her voice teasing but her eyes showing her real feelings. She was worried about my response.

I stroked her cheek. "Yeah, baby. I do."

Her smile was wide. "Then I'll have to start thinking about it."

I bent and captured her mouth. "You do that."

VI

I was surprisingly nervous the next few shifts, jumping at shadows and anxious when I was alone. Aldo made me call him when I arrived at the hotel, and he met me at my car and walked me to the deli. I also noticed he checked on me frequently. He had changed a little since the incident and our exchange. He was protective and close. I stayed with him a couple of nights, and the one night I insisted on going home, he showed up in the early hours of the morning, pulling me beside him onto the sofa and trapping me between the leather and his hard body. I managed to slide away, whispering I had to pee, for him to let me go, then I made coffee and sat and watched him sleep. In repose, his face was softer, less stern. His scruff was thick, his lips full, and he filled the sofa by himself, never mind when he had me pressed against him. He looked almost peaceful. Not quite—but more so than when he was awake and alert.

I wasn't sure what to make of his closeness. His protectiveness. I hoped it meant the same to him as it did to me. He was open, answering my questions as we lay together. He talked about his parents, losing them. Working with Roman. The vast scope of his businesses and the trust Roman placed in him. He made me laugh reciting the story of Luca and his fiancée/wife. The plans for their wedding to satisfy her family and keep peace.

Roman's reaction to it all.

I pulled a knee up to my chest, sipping my coffee. I glanced down with a frown. My big toe had a chip in the polish. I would have to redo my toenails today.

"I have a pedicure booked for you this morning," Aldo said, his voice gravelly from sleep.

I looked up, meeting his dark eyes. "Oh."

"And a massage. You're tense. I thought you'd enjoy it. You can head up to the room after and relax before your shift."

His caring and generosity touched me. "Thank you."

He sat up, stretching, the blanket falling to his waist. It showed all his muscles as they rippled while he moved. "We should have used the goddamn bed."

I laughed. "You're the one who pulled me to the sofa."

He stood, and I tried not to ogle him as he headed toward me, his cock already at attention. He stopped in front of me, taking my cup and draining it, then bending down and kissing me. I slid my hand between us, and he groaned. "Stop. Unless you want me to nail you on the floor or against the wall. That damn sofa wouldn't make it out alive once I start with you."

I laughed. It had protested loudly last night when he'd joined me on the sofa. I wasn't sure it would still be in one piece if he fucked me on it. The twin bed I'd bought wasn't much better. The noises it made when he lay on it were scary.

I slid to my knees. "There is a third option, big man."

He groaned loudly as I took him in my mouth.

"I love how your mind works."

I was more relaxed during my shift, my anxiety lessening as time went by. It had been a few nights since the incident with the asshole customer—or Ernest Morton, as I now knew his name to be. As I suspected, he had been reacting to whatever had been upsetting him at the moment and had no doubt moved on. Even if he could come back, I doubted he would. If I had acted that way, I would avoid the place it happened completely, far too embarrassed to show my face again. He probably regretted his behavior.

Aldo was covering tonight, so when I finished, I headed down to my car. As I approached it, I felt a shiver run through me. I looked around but noticed nothing out of the ordinary. A few other staff headed to their cars, the distant sound of other vehicles leaving on various levels. Nothing out of the ordinary, yet my nerves returned. I got to my car, unlocked it, and slid in. I turned to put my purse on the seat beside me and froze. Lying on the passenger seat was a dead rat. With the door shut, I could smell the putrid stench, and I grabbed at the door handle to open it, shocked when it wouldn't budge. Then I saw him. Standing next to the car, holding the door shut with the weight of his hands pressed on the metal. Ernest Morton.

"That's what happens to people who cross me," he said, loudly enough for me to hear through the glass. I covered my nose, the odor hitting me. I leaned on the horn, the sound loud in the garage. He leered at me, then let go, laughing as he strolled away.

I opened the door, stepping out, shaking.

I looked over at the rat, furious and upset. Obviously, I was wrong about him moving on. He was still angry.

But what kind of sicko did something like this?

I grabbed my phone and called Aldo. He answered right away, his voice concerned.

"Vi, baby—you okay?"

"N-no."

I could hear him running. "Where are you?"

"At my car."

"Five minutes."

He was there in four. He looked at me, in my car, and was on the phone, talking fast, his voice low and furious.

He hung up and pulled me into his arms. We waited only another couple of minutes. Aldo handed my keys to a younger man. "Get rid of it."

"Not my car," I gasped. "I need it."

"The rat," he explained. "And get the car detailed."

He tugged me close, and we headed to the elevator. "I'll take a cab home."

"You're staying here."

I didn't argue.

In the room, he poured us each a scotch, and he sat beside me. "Tell me exactly what happened."

I did and he listened. "You're parking in the VIP section from now on." He held up his hand before I could argue. "It's locked with security. And I'm going to find this asshole and teach him a lesson."

"What if—"

His raised brow silenced me.

"And you'll be escorted to and from your car. No arguments."

I didn't plan on arguing.

"I guess he was still pissed over the tweezer remark."

Aldo shook his head. "I checked him out. He has a temper. A few run-ins with the law. He's had a lot of jobs, and when I got my hands on his employment files, it showed anger issues and personality conflicts every time. He never lasts at a job long. He likes to gamble, and although he has some luck, he loses more than he makes most of the time. He'd had a bad night when he came to the deli. He'd been up and lost it all." He lifted a shoulder. "Some people just don't know when to walk away. He made a stupid bet against the house."

"How did you get hold of his employment files?"

He arched his eyebrow, refusing to answer.

"He'll be getting a visit. Personally."

"Aldo, you can't do anything to him."

"I can make sure he doesn't come near you again. I have no idea how he got in, except that he slipped in on the street level and was watching you to figure out which one was your car. We'll add more security."

"I hate to trouble—"

He cut me off, shaking his head. "Nothing can happen to you. I will not allow it."

"I'm sure now he's scared me, he'll move past it."

Aldo took my hands in his, staring down at them. "I will make sure he doesn't bother you again." He looked up and met my eyes. "I promise."

I smiled at him. "Okay."

ALDO

We couldn't locate Ernest Morton. He was no longer at his last known address. His landlord said he'd been evicted for nonpayment, and he hadn't seen him for over a month. I had a feeling he was in one of the old motels around town that took cash payments and no name. The tracker Roman had put on his car either failed, fell off, or he removed it. It had shut off the same night.

I was furious that he'd gotten to Vi. Scared her. I had her car detailed, and there was no smell or trace of the dead rat, but I noticed the look on her face every time she got in it. She had tossed a blanket over the passenger side seat, as if to cover it up. But I knew offering to buy her a new car would be met with resistance. I did convince her to stay at the hotel more often over the next couple of weeks. I had someone follow her home every night, and she did seem grateful for that.

She was incredibly strong and hated showing any weakness or vulnerability. But I saw it some days, lurking behind her eyes, shadowing her lovely irises. I didn't comment, only stayed closer on those days, letting her lean on me silently until she felt more herself. I was in awe of it most of the time. She refused to miss a day's work, and Wanda said she continued to be her best employee.

Roman seemed to like her a great deal. He started coming to the deli with me some nights, eating in the staff section and talking with Violet. They both had a dry sense of humor, and she made him laugh with her feistiness and lack of filter. She did wicked imitations of some casino staff, even his own bodyguards, and it tickled him. I had never seen him be as friendly to someone outside his circle, and when I pointed that out to him, his response was simple.

"She is part of your circle now, Aldo. Which grants her access to mine."

It was he who insisted I take her to meet Nonna V. I brought her to lunch one Sunday, more concerned about Nonna's opinion than I realized.

Nonna was gracious and seemed pleased to meet Vi. In fact, in ten minutes, they seemed to have forged a strong friendship, both of them teasing Roman and me.

"I want grandbabies, and these two do not cooperate," she lamented to Vi.

"Your other grandson is getting married," Vi pointed out. "He'll have to man up and do the job."

"I want more."

Vi shook her head sadly. "I've heard these two and their thoughts as to relationships and the future. I wouldn't hold my breath."

Nonna looked between us. "Why you stay with Aldo?"

"He's great—"

I cut her off, covering her mouth. "I'm good to her, Nonna V. We get on well."

Vi bit my hand, and I glared at her, pulling it away.

"As I was going to say, he is great to me and we understand each other," she said innocently, then winked at Nonna. "And he's great in the sack."

Nonna V laughed until she cried. Roman's laughter was loud, delighting in my discomfort. Yet, for some reason, I, too, was amused. Vi did that for me.

Roman liked to highlight all her good points.

He was as determined to find this asshole as I was, and he was frustrated by our lack of success. He offered a private car to take her to and from work, but she refused it. He offered her a twenty-four-hour bodyguard, and she laughed at him. She was incensed at his suggestions she'd be safer working the private dining area and informed him she didn't want to hang with the rich snobs, and that she belonged here with regular folks like her.

"Aldo is a rich snob," he said dryly. "You hang with him."

"No," she pointed out. "You're a rich snob. Aldo is just rich. I can handle that. But I'm with him for his dick, not his money."

Roman almost choked on his coffee, he laughed so hard.

So she stayed at Rolling Dice, and I watched her more than she realized. When she was out of my sight, I was anxious. I hated it when she went back to her apartment and I couldn't see her. Roman suggested I wire her place, but I knew she'd go ballistic. She agreed to a tracker in her purse, phone, and car. Anything else, she was against. In fact, after two weeks, she decided he was long gone.

"I think he's moved on, Aldo," she said at breakfast.

"I disagree."

She pushed back her hair with an annoyed huff. She'd been off the past couple of days, more tense than usual, quieter. "You said yourself that he has a track record of never staying in one place. He was pissed off over getting banned, and he scared me to get even. There've been zero sightings of him, no more garage incidents. Admit it, we need to go back to normal."

"Which means what?" I asked tersely.

"I go back to living my life. I live at my apartment and stay here on occasion. Not the other way around. I mean, it's a nice hotel room and all, but it's a hotel room, not a home."

"And your apartment is the Taj Mahal?" I snapped.

She frowned. "It's mine."

"I'll get you a bigger suite."

"I don't want a bigger suite, Aldo. I want to stop worrying about some asshole who has probably moved on and forgotten about me. Let's forget about him."

I rubbed my eyes. "Soon."

She looked at me for a moment. "Why?" she asked quietly.

"Why what?"

"Why are you so focused on this? You've done more than you have to."

"Because he got to you once. He could again."

"Or you could be overreacting. Compensating for something."

"Like what?" I demanded, not liking the direction this conversation had taken.

"Like trying to look after me to make up for the fact that you don't feel anything for me other than sexual."

I narrowed my eyes. "When have I said that?"

"With words, never. Not even gestures, really. You are generous and kind. Giving. You spoil me."

"I'd spoil you more if you would allow it."

"I'm not with you for your money or your gifts. But the truth is, you hold yourself back. Even more than I realized."

"What is it you want from me, Vi? I give you everything I'm capable of giving. Why are you suddenly dissatisfied?"

"I'm not dissatisfied," she replied. "I'm confused. Your actions and your words don't line up."

"What the hell does that mean?"

"You took me to meet Nonna V, someone you care about a great deal. You told Roman about us—we became friends. Or at least as friendly as one can get with Roman. The staff know. You have people watching over me. You're sweet and affectionate. Caring. Yet you don't let me in. You still hold me at arm's length. We're basically living together, yet we're not really a couple."

"You want me to spill all my secrets? Tell you my sordid past and all the hurts? Is that it? That's what you want?"

"I want to know all of you, Aldo. The good and bad. You won't scare me away."

I snorted in disbelief.

She sighed. "Relationships have to progress, or they die, Aldo. I know how I feel. I'm not sure you do—or if you're capable of expressing it."

Anger took over, fear driving it. Part of me worried about how she would feel if she knew everything. The violence of my past. That my future would always contain more of the same. That being with me, really being with me, meant she would be in danger. How thoughts of anything happening to her because of me niggled at me with worry. How the feelings I had for her frightened me. They were unlike anything I had ever experienced. She had become more than I ever expected.

And being an idiot, instead of expressing my fears, I let anger get the best of me.

"Relationship? When did this progress to a relationship? We're fuckmates, Vi. We agreed to that. Just because I look after you doesn't mean I'm looking to marry you—or even 'progress,' as you stated, into something resembling a relationship."

She stared at me, and I saw the flash of hurt she tried to hide.

"If I'm just a fuckmate, Aldo, you need not expend so much energy on my behalf. I can look after myself quite well."

"Yes, *so well.* Your boyfriend ripped you off and you never noticed that your best friend was sleeping with him before they stole everything you owned, if I'm not mistaken. Then you have to mouth off and anger an already pissed-off patron so he comes after you. I had no choice but to try to keep you safe. You're my employee."

There was no disguising her hurt this time. My words hit her hard. Her voice was thick when she responded.

"And that is all I am? An employee you enjoy fucking?"

"Stop putting words in my mouth!"

She stood. "Someone needs to help you talk, Aldo. You have no idea how to express your feelings. I guess being a tough guy is easier for you than being real."

I flung my napkin down and stood as well. "I'm done with this conversation."

"Of course you are."

"I'll see you later."

"I'm going to my place tonight."

I hated that. I detested she had a place to go. I was furious we were fighting. That her words struck something inside me. I despised the fact that she was right on so many levels. And I really loathed the fact that I wanted her to stay and make me talk to her.

"Whatever. Terry will escort you to your car and follow you home."

And I walked out.

CHAPTER 14
ALDO

My phone rang as I was leaving the high-roller area. One of our VIPs was upset over his missing parking pass, insisting it had been in his pocket when he'd left home. He informed me a man had bumped into him on the street, and he was certain it had been stolen. I assured him we would cancel it and provide him a new one, and I was on my way to arrange it so I could get downstairs and see Vi before she left. I didn't want her to leave still angry. I wanted a chance to talk to her.

I answered quickly, seeing it was Gordon from the security area. I had been in a shitty mood all day after my fight with Vi. I'd had to stop myself from going to the suite a dozen times during the day and talking to her. I'd been short with Roman and everyone around me. I hoped I could keep my temper for whatever situation Gordon was calling about.

"What?"

"The facial recognition just picked up on Morton's face. He was trying to avoid cameras, but we caught him."

"Where?" I snapped, picking up my pace. Roman glanced my way, matching my hurried footsteps.

"He was on the main floor, but he stepped into the elevators. He went down."

The parkade. The missing pass. It was too coincidental to be an accident.

Vi would be getting off in ten minutes. I had to stop her from going to her car.

I hung up, calling the deli. Wanda answered, sounding chipper. "Rolling Dice, how may I help?"

"Wanda," I barked. "Violet. Don't let her leave."

"She left about ten minutes ago. It's quiet and she had a headache, so I sent her home."

"Was Terry outside?"

"No, he just showed up. He was about to call you."

"Fuck!" I roared and began to run.

VI

My head pounded, and I was grateful Wanda had let me go early, even ten minutes. It was rare I got a headache, but when I did, they knocked me out for a bit. I needed to get home before the pain was too much and I couldn't drive. I didn't even wait for Terry. I was going to my car and leaving. Aldo could fuck off. He had basically told me I was good enough to fuck but not to have a relationship with. If I wasn't good enough to have a relationship with, then he didn't get the right to act all cavemanish on me, and I was done with it all. That asshole who'd hassled me hadn't been seen for weeks. He had been scared away and wasn't coming back to seek revenge on a waitress in a deli. He'd had his fun and was over it. I was certain of it.

I approached my car, feeling weary and drained. Aldo's words had hurt me earlier. More than I had expected his rejection to. My feelings for him ran deeper than I had admitted to myself, and hearing his cold interpretation of our situation had stung. I knew it meant I would have to leave sooner than I thought. I couldn't work here and see him every day, knowing he would move on and I would still love him. I had a feeling I would love him for the rest of my life. The thought of seeing him with another woman made me feel ill.

I dug in my pocket for the keys, not paying attention to the garage around me. It was only when I got to my car and attempted to put the key in the lock that I realized how quiet it seemed. Normally, other people were leaving and I would hear voices echoing across the garage, but tonight, I was early so it was deserted. And the light closest to my car was burned out, which was odd since the VIP section was always taken care of. You needed a special pass to get on to this floor of the parkade, and only Aldo, Roman, and a few other people had access to this section.

A shiver went through me. I had stopped being nervous in the garage, but suddenly, everything in me kicked into high gear and my anxiety hit me. I closed my hand around my cell phone and gripped my keys tightly. Unexpectedly, I was pushed from behind, and I fell to my knees with a cry of pain when the cement dug into my bare skin.

Rough hands grabbed my neck, squeezing. I was dragged to my feet and spun around, then slammed into the hard wall behind me. I struggled to fight against the hands pinning me to the concrete, but my attacker had his fingers wrapped around my biceps in a hard, painful grip.

I lifted my eyes and met the malevolent gaze of Ernest Morton. He was close enough I could smell the alcohol on his breath and his unwashed skin. But it was the cold, calculated look on his face that frightened me. His mouth was twisted in satisfaction, his eyes dark and foreboding.

"Got ya," was all he said. It was enough. I knew, without a doubt, I wasn't going to be leaving this garage alive. Tears sprang to my eyes, fear coursing through my veins, my heartbeat galloping in my chest.

He grinned. "Not so tough without your bodyguards, are you?" He leaned closer. "You got me banned from my hunting ground, bitch. You have to pay for that."

I struggled against him, attempting to kick and push him away. But he held me too tightly to the wall, angling his body away to stop my attempts to hit him. Then he pressed an arm to my neck, leaning on it, cutting off my breath.

"I wanted to take you somewhere and have fun, but I don't have time. Shame." He pressed harder, and I began to fight in earnest. I managed to kick him, and he cursed, his hold on my neck loosening. I kicked again and broke free, managing to get a scream out before he grabbed me, throwing me to the cement. My head hit the ground with a loud crack, and everything dimmed around me. He rolled me over, straddling me, pushing me down. My back protested at the weight of him, the feeling of the concrete tearing at my skin. He wrapped his hands around my neck and began to tighten them. Between his weight on top of me and the pressure on my neck, all my air was cut off. He sat on my arms, pinning them down, and I had no way to fight him. No way to save myself. I struggled against the pain and the darkness, filled with sadness and horror. Aldo's face flashed behind my eyes, and I regretted my anger the last time I'd seen him. The words I had flung at him. I kept my eyes shut, wanting to see his face, and not the face of the man killing me, as I died.

Except I heard a roar. Like a freight train, growing louder, and my eyes flew open in time to see Morton's head lift up in shock. There was a blur and his head snapped back, and he fell away from me onto the concrete.

There were voices, yelling, talking, and a man bent over me. Aldo stared down at me in abject horror. "Baby," he whispered. "Oh God, Vi."

All I could do was stare.

Aldo kept speaking to me. He never took his eyes off my face. Bending, he lifted me into his arms, cursing as I whimpered in pain.

"I need a car. Now!"

A voice I recognized spoke. "It's waiting. So is Sims. I'll take care of this."

"He's mine to finish," Aldo growled.

"I know."

Aldo began to move, the motion making me groan as fire rushed over my back and arms. “I’m sorry. I have to get you to a doctor,” he said, his voice faint in my ears.

“Please,” I whimpered. “Help.”

“I have you, Vi. I promise.”

“Sorry,” I mumbled. “Didn’t mean…”

It was too much effort to finish, but he pressed a kiss to my temple. “I know, baby. I know.”

Then I was out.

ALDO

Nothing prepared me for the terror of rounding the corner and seeing that asshole on top of Vi, strangling her. I let out a roar, all the anger and frustration of weeks coming out.

I rushed toward him, kicking him directly in the face when he looked up, shocked. He fell backward onto the dirty floor of the garage. Roman and Terry dragged him away, making sure he didn’t get up. Bending over Vi, I was horrified to see her injuries.

Her clothes were torn, bruising already appearing on her legs and arms. Dark fingerprints were embedded into the delicate skin of her throat. When I lifted her head, there was blood on my fingers. Red painted my vision, matching her injuries. She cried out softly when I lifted her. Roman already had a car waiting, and he knew what I meant when I told him Morton was mine. Roman could have some time with him first, but I got the pleasure of seeing his life drain from his eyes. He would pay for every bruise, every mark on Vi's skin.

At the hospital, I found it hard to release her from my arms. She had been in and out on the journey, whimpering in pain at times, her anguish feeding my anger. Her blood seeped through my fingers and ran down my arm. But I kept my temper. My fury was not directed at her, but at myself and Morton. I said things I hadn't meant to keep her away from me, and the thought of her dying, thinking I didn't care, was eating at me. I had been a total asshole, and I knew without a doubt Vi would tell me my words hurt her more than what Morton had done to her. I regretted every word that had come from my mouth earlier. Every single one was a lie, shouted to cover up my fear of loving her.

I swore I would rectify that as soon as she woke up.

Dr. Sims rushed her into an exam room, and I stood in the hall, lost and in agony.

I had never experienced fear like this. My chest felt like it was being crushed by the pain. I couldn't bear the thought of the terror she must have felt, being attacked. The pain she went through. The pain she was going to go through to heal. But she wasn't going to go through it on her own.

I had let her down once, and I wasn't going to do it again.

And I was going to make sure the man who hurt her would never have the chance to do it again. Come morning, she would be safe with me, and he would no longer exist.

Until then, he would wish he were dead.

I would make sure of it.

VI

I woke up, the room around me dim and unfamiliar. My head throbbed, my body ached, and my throat felt as if it was on fire. I lifted my head, the pain making me whimper. A man in the corner came forward, and I was confused, the face not the one I expected to see.

"Roman?" I managed to get out of my painful throat.

He frowned and nodded, lifting the water glass to my lips. It hurt to swallow, but I got some of the cool liquid down. He studied me, shaking his head and pressing the call button. I was so bewildered—feeling dazed and unsure. And the pain was overwhelming. A white-coated man came in, introducing himself as Dr. Sims. He asked me some questions. My name. The date. The time of day. I was a little fuzzy on that one, but I guessed night. He pointed to Roman and asked me to identify him. "Roman the Warrior," I whispered. Aldo often called him that, saying he was constantly at war with something or someone, always fighting for what he wanted or believed in.

It sort of suited him.

Roman grunted, and Dr. Sims smiled. "Close enough."

He explained my injuries, but I had trouble following him. I heard the words concussion and trauma. Contusions and bruising. Pain meds and rest. I could only nod. His voice drifted off, and I realized I had dozed. I blinked, meeting Roman's steady green gaze.

I didn't understand why he was here. Where was Aldo? My heartbeat picked up. Had he left me? Or, worse, was he hurt?

I grabbed at Roman's arm. "Aldo," was all I could say.

I had heard employees talk about Roman. Cold. Removed. Stern. Disciplined. Scary. All were words used to describe him. But his gaze was kind as he patted my hand. "Aldo is fine. The doctor didn't expect you to wake up for a few more hours. Aldo, ah, had some unfinished business to take care of. He left me with you to make sure you were watched over and, in case you woke up, saw a friendly face." He grinned widely, showing off his teeth, trying to be silly. "Is that friendly enough?"

I had to smile at his attempt. Comedy was not his forte.

"Where?"

He shook his head. "Don't ask questions you don't want answers to, Violet."

"Is Ernest dead?"

Roman frowned and paused, as if trying to decide how truthful to be. "If not, he soon will be. You will never have to fear him again. No woman will."

"What?"

He leaned closer, keeping his voice low and steady. "We watched the camera feed. Listened to what he said to you in the parking garage. About blocking him from his hunting ground. My people did some digging, and I got some information from one of my sources at the police station. We matched up dates he was at the casino with times women were attacked close to it or when they arrived home. The police will be getting a file, and I have a feeling it will solve a lot of open cases." He smirked. "We'll even make sure DNA is provided."

"How?"

This time, his grin was evil. "We'll lend a hand, so to speak."

He said it in the same tone of voice as one would use to say they dropped off a pie to a friend who had been grateful to receive it. Pleased and satisfied. Calm. Nothing suggesting what I knew he meant.

"Aldo isn't hurt?"

"No. He's fine. He'll be pissed he wasn't here when you woke up, but ending this was important to him. He had to be the one."

"We had a fight."

Roman sat back, nodding. "I know. He told me. He blames himself, and if it's any consolation, he was coming to see you before this happened. He hated fighting with you."

A tear slipped down my cheek. "I have to go."

"Go *where*?" he asked, leaning forward. "You're in no condition to get out of bed."

"I have to leave Niagara Falls."

He looked shocked. “Why?”

I had no idea why I was confiding in Roman. It had to be the meds messing with my head. “I love him, and he’ll never love me back. I can’t stay and watch him be with someone else.” I winced as a fresh wave of pain washed over me.

He leaned to the right and tapped a button on the machine that was beeping. “That will help. Probably knock you out soon too.” He hunched forward. “So, listen to me carefully. I have never seen Aldo care for someone the way he cares for you. You make him different. Better. He laughs and smiles. The same way Luca does because of Justine. He might not be able to say the words yet, but he feels them, Violet. Give him time. What happened tonight has shaken him. He was a man possessed when I got here. Terrified of losing you. You mean more than you know. More than he knows. Don’t walk away from him. I swear it will end him.”

I stared at him, the medicines doing their job and easing the pain, but clouding my train of thought. Was Roman saying Aldo was in love with me?

“Yes, he is,” he responded as if I had asked him that out loud.

Maybe I had.

I blinked, trying to fight off the exhaustion that was bearing down on me. “Thank you,” I mumbled.

He leaned even closer. "I'll let you in on another little secret, Vi. I like you. You're smart and funny and exactly what Aldo needs. Strong. Feisty. A fighter. He needs that. I think you'll love him perfectly. Exactly the way he needs."

"I like you too. You're not so tough."

He laughed lowly. "Not all the time. I have my moments."

"You love him," I said, my voice a little slurry.

"Aldo? Yes. Like a brother. Him, Luca, Nonna. They are my family. I have a feeling you will be too." He patted my hand. "Just give him some time."

"Okay."

Sleep was pulling at me. "Roman?"

"Yeah, Vi?"

"Did you hit him—the asshole, I mean? Did you hit him hard?"

"Like a ton of fucking bricks."

"Thank you."

And I was out.

CHAPTER 15
VI

The next time I woke up fully, Aldo was there. I knew it before I opened my eyes. I felt him. His presence. I could hear him talking, the low timbre of his voice reaching my ears. I heard Roman as well and another voice—the doctor, I thought, but I wasn't sure.

"She'll rest better there."

"You should leave her until the morning," the unfamiliar voice said.

"It is morning. It's four a.m.," Aldo said dryly.

"Is she in danger?" Roman asked, sounding like the voice of reason.

"She needs to be watched. We're monitoring her here."

I recalled being woken a few times. A gentle voice asking me questions before I was allowed to fall asleep again. Each time, I was given some water to sip. I needed some of that now.

"I'll ask again. If I take her, is she in danger?"

"I want her here."

"Fine. Then I'm staying."

"Aldo?" I called, although my voice sounded more like a whisper. A rough one at that.

He was beside me quickly. "Vi, baby, I'm right here."

I blinked open my eyes and met his dark, penetrating gaze.

"Thirsty," I managed to get out.

He pressed the water cup to my mouth, and I sipped, grateful as the cool water helped soothe the burn in my throat. He stepped aside so the doctor could examine me, but Aldo kept his gaze locked with mine and his hand on my arm.

Dr. Sims straightened. "All looks good."

"So, she can go?"

The doctor sighed. "In eight hours. I want another CT scan, and if she is okay at noon, you can take her."

Aldo nodded, looking grim. Roman gripped his arm and said something to him. Then he turned to me and offered me a smile. He touched my cheek. "I'll see you later, doll. Remember what I said?"

I nodded cautiously since it hurt to move my head too much.

Aldo glared at him, and Roman laughed and left with the doctor. I sighed as I felt Aldo cup my face. "What do you need?"

"Nothing."

"Are you in pain?"

"Is he dead?"

Aldo looked startled.

"I know you were gone. I woke up, and Roman told me."

He looked displeased, so I asked again. "Is he dead?"

"Very. I made sure of it."

"How?"

"Vi—"

I interrupted him. "How?"

He leaned over me, rage simmering in his gaze. "First, with my hands until he begged, and then I shot him.

Six times. I started with his feet. I ended with his head."

I should have been horrified. He had murdered a man. Brutally.

But instead, all I felt was grateful.

"Roman got in a few rounds too," he added. "He was already suffering when I got there. I added to it."

I sighed and shut my eyes. "Thank you."

I felt his touch on my face. "Don't be afraid of me, baby. I would never hurt you."

"I'm not afraid."

I swallowed the lump forming in my throat, but I got the words out before I fell asleep.

"I love you."

ALDO

I stared down at Violet, her injuries screaming and feeding my anger. I had never known such rage. The instinct to protect, to kill what was hurting the person I loved, was as penetrating as it was powerful. But the person responsible for her pain was dead—at my hands. I had made sure he suffered, felt the same fear as she no doubt had when he'd attacked her. But I didn't give him any false hope that he would make it through the night. I had picked him apart piece by piece, breaking bones, tearing flesh until he was a quivering mass of pain in front of me. I got the names of other women he had hurt and had Gordon run them through our members' player passes. The fact that he had used this casino and business as a hunting ground had already earned him a painful, prolonged session with Roman. I would make sure the other women he had hurt or terrified found out the man who had caused it was dead and they had nothing to fear. All the names would go to our contact at the police department, along with the hand I'd cut off as he screamed. I planned to make sure all the women were compensated somehow—something to help them rebuild their lives. I knew Roman would want to be part of the gesture, and although the women would never know where it came from, we would rest easier.

What was left of him was being cremated, then would be taken to the dump. He didn't deserve a burial or to be remembered. He had no family, no friends, and no one to mourn him.

His presence and memory would be wiped away.

I sat down, looking at Vi, hating the fact that she was there, lying in a hospital bed. Wishing I could hurt him again. I wondered if she would still love me if she knew how I'd tortured him. How I had killed other people.

Would those sweet words still fall from her mouth? Would she look at me the same way?

I had never seen someone look at me the way she did. With absolute trust. Adoration. Her face lit up when she saw me. My heart sped up every time I captured a glimpse of her.

Did hers do the same?

Was I really capable of love?

Was that what this emotion I felt every time I saw her, every time I thought about her, was?

Love?

I scrubbed my hands over my face. I watched her chest rise and fall in slumber. The pain medication they were giving her was helping her rest. I matched my breathing to hers, slowly feeling calmer. I slid my hand over hers, a smile breaking out on my face when she flipped her hand and entwined our fingers, while still sleeping. I studied her, my plans in place for the next while. Roman knew I wasn't going to be around much for a few days, and he assured me he had it covered.

"She's special," he said quietly when I arrived and found him seated beside her, answering emails on his phone.

"Did she wake up?"

"Yes. We talked a little. She is…" He smiled. "She is your other half, Aldo."

I frowned, and he placed his hand on my shoulder. "You deserve it. You deserve her."

"I just murdered a man in cold blood and enjoyed it. What kind of person does that?"

"A man protecting the woman he loves. It is part of the world we inhabit, Aldo. It doesn't change the man you are. You are, I think, exactly what she needs." He paused. "She is exactly what you need. Take care of her. Talk to her."

"And tell her what when she asks?" I questioned. "Because she is going to ask."

"She already did, and I told her. She was grateful. To both of us."

That surprised me.

"She knows who you are. She still loves you. She told me that."

"The two of you were having a good gab session about feelings, were you?" I asked.

He grinned. "Pain meds tend to make people talkative. And frankly, I was glad they did. I like her, Aldo. I like her a lot. Don't fuck this up."

I didn't have a chance to retort since Dr. Sims had walked in, and shortly after, Vi woke up.

But now as I sat and watched her, I knew he was right. She was special, and she was mine. She was also hurt and needed my care, and she would have that.

My phone buzzed with a message, and I saw it was Roman.

BTW, I added to the guest list—you and a plus-one for the wedding. It's in ten days, so she should be well enough to come. Luca is thrilled. He can't wait to meet her. And you should take her to see Nonna again. I might have mentioned your new relationship status to her.

I had no response aside from a rude icon I sent him. I knew the bastard was laughing at me, enjoying all this. I sent him a return message.

ME

Wait until it is your turn. I am going to have a shit-ton of fun at your expense.

ROMAN

Will never happen.

ME

Never say never, you smug prick. I'll remind you of this one day.

He returned my rude icon, and I set aside my phone, then picked it up again. I had things that needed to happen, and I needed help.

VI

I woke up to the sun filling the hospital room. Aldo was beside me, his head bent as he frowned at something on his phone. I cleared my sore throat, and he looked up, instantly alert. He slid his phone into his pocket and leaned over closer to me. His expression was unreadable, but his eyes were a mass of emotions. Far too many to understand.

"Hey baby, how are you feeling?"

"Sore. Thirsty."

"I got you this." He placed a straw in my mouth, and I sipped the icy cold mango smoothie. It was delicious and felt good on my throat. He smiled as I gripped the cup, pulling it from his hands.

"Take it slow," he advised.

I sipped the delicious beverage.

"When you're done, they'll check you out and discharge you."

"It's noon?"

He chuckled. "You remembered hearing that, did you?"

"Bits and pieces. Did I pass the CT?"

"Yes, and it's almost twelve. I'll take you home—you'll be more comfortable." He paused. "My place."

I nodded in agreement. "The hotel will be more comfortable."

He shook his head. "My house. I'm taking you to my house."

I stopped sipping and looked at him. "Why?"

"Because I can care for you there easier. You'll have the privacy and space you need to heal." He cleared his throat. "As long as you're okay with that."

"Are you sure?" I asked. "You've never—I mean, I didn't think—"

He smiled and tapped my cheek. "I'm sure, baby. It's time. More than time, really. I want you to see where I'm just Aldo. See how you feel about him."

I took his hand, feeling the rough edges of his fingers. The heat of his skin. The way he wrapped his large palm around mine protectively. Carefully.

"I'd like that."

"Good. I got some of your things brought over. Brian and Fran know you're staying with me. Your shifts are covered for the next while. I've handled everything." He fixed me with a look. "Even the tip-sharing for Derek. You should have told me about that. I would have helped."

"It was my thing, not yours."

"Well, he is covered. Tips and extra hours." He smiled at me, tenderness softening his face. "You're too good a person for me, Vi."

"No. We're perfect for each other."

He stood, then kissed me softly. "I'll tell the doc you're ready."

I watched him go, worry and pain battling for dominance. Aldo seemed too calm. Was he really okay?

What did his taking me to his house signify? Was it as important a step as I thought, or was he reacting to my being attacked?

I shut my eyes with a sigh, pain winning out. It was all too much to think about. I would figure it out later.

Aldo took charge, making me realize how powerful he was. In moments, all the equipment was disconnected, discharge papers procured, and before I knew what was happening, Aldo gathered me into his arms and proceeded to walk toward the exit.

"You can't carry me," I hissed at him.

"Why?"

"I'm too tall to be carried like a child."

He laughed. "I think we're doing just fine. Stop squirming and relax."

I laid my head against his shoulder. I had to admit, it felt nice being cradled in his arms. I felt safe and cared for—and oddly small held against his broad chest.

I wasn't used to feeling small.

He held me in the car all the way to his house. I dozed off and on, waking as he stepped from the vehicle. I gazed at the Victorian-style house in awe from the safety of his arms. I was still woozy enough to allow him to carry me inside.

Inside, Aldo set me down, and I looked around in wonder. The rooms were large and filled with sun. Wide planked floors, wood trim, and pocket doors were set off in a soft caramel color. The fireplace was incredible, with beautiful stone and a mantel that gleamed in the light.

I looked at Aldo. "It is amazing."

He smiled. "Living and dining room. Kitchen and a den. Upstairs, three bedrooms. And my favorite place in the house."

I walked slowly to the kitchen, marveling at the black cupboards and beautiful counters. The same wooden floors were in every room.

With a smile, he opened a door at the back of the kitchen, and I gasped in delight. "An elevator?"

He chuckled. "The owners installed it when she fell and broke a hip and the stairs were too much. I didn't take it out. It's rather fun."

He took us up to the second floor and waved at the two doors on either side of the hall. "Bedrooms." Then he led me into the primary bedroom. Spacious, airy, with an incredible view of the Niagara River from the large windows, the room also had a balcony you could sit on and enjoy the view. The whole house was done in simple creams, caramels, and offset by dark wood. A few splashes of color popped up here and there, but for the most part, it was a blank canvas.

"Aldo, it is spectacular. Why don't you spend more time here?"

He shrugged. "I am planning on it over the next few days. You need to get back into bed."

"Not until I have showered."

"Vi, you've lost the little color you had in your cheeks, and you're swaying on your feet. Bed. Now."

"I can't."

"Why?"

I clutched his arm. "I smell him. I want it off. Please."

He went tense and nodded curtly. He led me to the bathroom, turning on the multiheaded shower and stripping out of his clothes. I frowned at him, and he simply huffed. "You are not getting in there alone. You look as if you're going to fall over any second."

I had to admit I felt that way. My head ached and I was weak. I hated feeling so feeble. I allowed him to help me undress, and I caught a glimpse of myself in the mirror. My neck was black and blue, with bruising all around the base. My eyes were red. I turned, gasping at the sight of my back. It was as darkly bruised as my neck, with long scratches from the concrete wall and floor. My arms showed the trauma as well. My knees were scraped and sore. So were my hands. I met Aldo's eyes in the mirror, the fury in them hot and burning, his fists clenched. He saw my distress and laid his hands on my shoulders, his touch gentle.

"I wish I could kill him all over again," he muttered.

I shook my head. "I need you right now, Aldo."

"You have me."

He ushered me into the shower, blocking the spray and adjusting it so it didn't hit my back directly. He didn't let me do a thing, soaping me carefully and washing my hair, taking great care not to touch the area where I had been hurt. His tenderness did something to me, eased my tension, and I found myself crying silently as he continued his ministrations. He tilted up my face, frowning when he realized I was sobbing. He froze. "Am I hurting you, baby?"

"No," I managed to whisper. "It-it's just all…" I had no idea how to finish that sentence.

"I understand. Cry as much as you need, but make sure you cry with me. Don't hide it."

Those words only made me cry more. He kept tending to me, talking quietly until he was done. He made me sit on the bench in the shower as he washed, handling his own body far rougher than he had mine. When he reached for the shampoo, I picked up the bottle. "Let me. Please."

He kneeled in front of me, and I washed his thick locks, ignoring the dull ache in my hands, enjoying the action of massaging his head, hoping it felt good. He stood and rinsed, shutting off the water flow. He dried me off, rubbing some ointment into my back. I tried not to flinch, but I knew I did, and he looked grim as he finished. He pulled a loose T-shirt over my head and handed me some pills.

He dried off and pulled on some sweats, then led me to his room, drawing back the covers. "I had everything cleaned, so you'll be comfortable. Do you want me to close the curtains?"

"Please."

He did so using a remote, and the room became dark.

"Will you stay?"

"If you want me to."

"Please."

He lay beside me. My back was too sore to press on, so I turned on the side that hurt the least. He moved closer, wrapping an arm around me. Our chests melded together, and I felt the heat of him soak into me.

"Is this okay?"

"Yes." I patted his chest. "I'm not afraid of you, Aldo. I like your touch."

He pulled my head to his torso, his fingers stroking my neck in soft passes. We were quiet for a moment, then I spoke. “I’m sorry.”

“For what?”

“I should have waited for Terry. I had a headache, and I was angry. But I shouldn’t have left.”

He sighed, his breath warm on my head. “I’m sorry for what I said that made you angry. I was being an ass. I didn’t mean it, Violet. I was reacting, not speaking the truth. You do mean something. Something big. I’m trying to sort it all out. I was coming to you when I got the call.”

He was silent for a moment. “I’ve never experienced fear the way I did when I realized he had gotten to you. That I had failed to protect you. That I might never have the chance to tell you I was sorry and that I cared so much it frightened me.”

I lifted my head, meeting his eyes. “When he was choking me, all I could think about was I would never get the chance to tell you that I loved you. That you would never know how happy you made my life and that I would never regret a moment I spent with you. I was so sad that you would never know how incredible I think you are.”

His eyes glittered in the dimness of the room. I was shocked to realize he was crying.

"I don't deserve that."

"Yes. Yes, you do."

He pressed a kiss to my forehead. "I will try to live up to your expectations of me."

"You already do."

He tugged me a little closer, and I had to shut my eyes. He didn't tell me that he loved me back, but I remembered what Roman had said. I needed to give Aldo time.

A small part of me wondered if he ever would.

And that part of me cried.

CHAPTER 16
VI

The next few days passed by in a blur. I slept a lot, often only waking because the pain broke my sleeping pattern. Every time I woke up, Aldo was there, ever patient, wanting to help. He fed me, gave me medication, helped me in the shower, and held me when he would tuck me back into bed. A few times, I roused alone, only to see him sitting in the chair close to the bed, watching me or dozing. A couple of times, he had his laptop open and was busy typing. Twice, he was on the phone with Roman, or least I assumed that's who it was. I caught snippets of the conversation, but my mind was too tired to link it all together, and I would fall back asleep.

I woke up again, my mind more alert and the pain not as intense. I blinked in the midmorning light, glancing at the clock. It was past eleven, and I was surprised to find myself alone in the room. It was the first time that had happened since Aldo had brought me here. He was always close when I woke.

I felt a breeze coming in the window, and I sat up gingerly, breathing in the fresh air. I could hear the timbre of Aldo's voice, and I swung my legs over the mattress and stood. I had to take a minute to find my equilibrium, then I walked to the open window and peeked out. Aldo was in the front of his house, pacing as he spoke. He looked serious, his voice pitched low. I couldn't really hear what he was saying, but I was glad to know he was close. I padded to the bathroom, emptying my bladder, washing my hands and face, and brushing my teeth. I still looked pale, and the bruises were dark on my skin, but my head was clearer and the persistent headache was a dull thump instead of a semi crashing inside my head. I was happy to be upright.

I found a bag of my clothes, and I pulled on some sweats and a shirt, stopping for a moment to catch my breath. I headed downstairs slowly, marveling at the beautiful woodwork and old-fashioned charm of the house. In the kitchen, I found a pot of coffee and poured a cup, almost salivating at the scent. The first sip hit me just right, and I almost groaned in delight as I swallowed. I sat down on one of the stools at the large island and looked around with fresh eyes. It was a beautiful house. Decorated simply, but with great taste. But it looked like a hotel—nothing personal or out of place.

The front door opened, and Aldo headed toward the stairs, stopping in shock at seeing me sitting in the kitchen. He crossed the room, standing right in front of me. "You're up. Out of bed."

"Drinking coffee," I added.

He cupped my face, cradling it in his hands. He bent forward and kissed me. It was his signature move whenever he greeted me, I realized. It was how he showed his deep affection. I savored the pressure of his mouth on mine, the way his tongue slid inside and tangled with mine. Gently, with great care, and yet so passionately, it stole my breath.

He eased back, resting his forehead on mine. "Hey, baby. It's good to see you in my kitchen."

"Hi, big man." I turned and kissed his palm. "It's a nice kitchen."

He laughed and drew back. "How are you feeling?"

"Better. My head is clearer."

"Good."

"And I'm hungry."

"Even better. I'll make us breakfast."

But he didn't move, still holding my face and looking at me. His expression was tormented, his eyes saying so much.

"Don't," I whispered. "We have to move on, Aldo. Don't blame yourself, and don't dwell. I went to the parking lot alone. I shouldn't have."

"Because you were angry with me after I behaved like an asshole."

"And I forgive you. You forgive me for going without an escort. Then we can move on."

"Just like that?"

"Just like that."

His hands tightened. "I want to progress, Vi. We do have a relationship." He swallowed. "An important one." He locked his eyes with mine. "I need to find the right words."

I slipped my hands around his wrists. "I'll wait."

He nodded and pressed his lips to mine again, then stepped back. "Breakfast," he said.

"And more coffee."

His smile was wide. "Anything you want, baby."

We had breakfast, and afterward, Aldo escorted me upstairs using the elevator since I refused to allow him to carry me. He took me to the top floor, showing me his favorite place in the house.

"This is what sold it to me," he explained.

I looked around at the room in awe. Wood lined the floors, ceiling, and walls, making it cozy. Windows were on either end, showing the views. The front looked over the river. The back, his yard which led onto a field, the wild grasses blowing lazily in the breeze.

There was a small fireplace. A big TV hung on one wall. A large sofa sat across from it, and a huge chair was in the corner. It was warm and homey. Lived-in. Aldo had piles of books scattered everywhere. Some puzzles were on the shelf. A cozy rug made me curl my toes on the softness under my feet.

"The windows are treated," he said. "I can see out, but even with the lights on, you can't see in. I love to watch the river. Sit and see the storms in the summer. The snow in the winter. It's a place I can unwind. Relax."

"Do you do that enough?" I asked.

"No," he admitted. "But I may have found a reason to do it more often." He looped his arm around my waist, drawing me close. "You like it, Vi?"

"I love it." I walked toward the back windows. "Your yard is large."

"The couple who owned it loved to garden. I don't have time, so they're overgrown, but one day…"

"I always loved to garden," I admitted. "I find it relaxing. You don't get that in Toronto."

He laughed. "Nope."

"I always dreamed of a house with a garden. A place to grow. To have my own home, you know?" I said quietly. "A place to belong."

"I hear you."

"It's lovely, Aldo. Thank you for showing it to me."

"I want you to use it. Be up here with me. Come up on your own if I'm out. Enjoy it."

"You must have to go to the casino."

"Tomorrow."

"Aldo, I'm fine. Much better."

"Good. I'll go tomorrow. Roman is covering. We'll figure out a schedule for the next while." He paused. "I don't want you alone."

I turned and faced him. "But you said he was dead."

"He is. But you went through something awful. I need to stay close."

His words touched me, and I decided not to argue. "All right."

He touched my cheek. "Luca is getting married next Saturday. I would like you to come with me."

"Roman's brother," I confirmed.

"Yes. It will be quite the affair."

"Oh, ah…" I trailed off. "I'm not sure I have the appropriate dress for something that fancy."

"We'll figure that out, if you want to go."

I touched my neck, unsure.

"We can cover them, baby. I want you with me."

I squared my shoulders. "Yes."

He kissed me softly. "Thank you." Gently, he tugged me over to the sofa. "Nap time, I think."

I didn't argue.

Each day, I felt stronger. More myself. But Aldo was right, and when he left me alone the first time, my nerves kicked in. I jumped at every sound, checked, and rechecked the locks, and when he called me to see how I was, he knew and came directly home. I felt like a child as he wrapped his arms around me, and I leaned on him, relief flowing through me at his touch.

"I'm sorry."

"I shouldn't have left you."

"I know he's gone. I know I'm safe," I babbled, unable to explain my anxiety.

"It's okay, baby. I'm here," he crooned.

"I'm sorry," I repeated.

He drew back, cupping my face and kissing me. I instantly felt calmer. "I'm here," he whispered. "Everything is okay."

I nestled against him. As long as he was close, he was right. "Okay."

Roman showed up the next day, carrying flowers and a tray of lasagna from his nonna. I was surprised to see him.

"Does Aldo know you're here?"

He nodded. "I told him I would drop by. I know he was worried about leaving you in the evening. He said yesterday was rough, so I thought I would help. I told him I would cover later so he could come home, but I thought you might like the company. My nonna's lasagna is not to be missed. She'll come see you soon."

He sat down. "How are you?"

"Getting better every day."

"You're coming to the wedding, right?"

"Yes." I touched my neck. "I think so."

He nodded in understanding. "They'll fade. A dress can cover them."

"I have to find one."

He waved me off. "I'll send the manager of my boutique over to you. Gerry will find you something."

"That is incredibly kind," I said, sliding a cup of coffee toward him.

"It's easy to be kind to people I like," he replied with a wink. "Especially the one my right hand is in love with."

A small thrill ran through me at his words, but I didn't comment.

"Tell me about Aldo and you when you were younger."

He was silent for a moment. "My upbringing was rough after my mother died. My father was determined to make us over into him. There was a lot of darkness around me. He celebrated the bad stuff and constantly pitted Luca and me against each other. My only light was my nonna. And Aldo. He was the one person I could be Roman with. We'd sneak away and do kid stuff. Stupid things. Daring each other who could jump off the highest tree. Dive underwater and hold our breath the longest. He, Luca, and I would do all sorts of idiotic things when my father wasn't around. We were just us then. My father thought he was winning, but what he did was make us closer. We hated his business. His ways of doing things. The constant violence. He loved it. I loathed it, even though it is a part of me. Luca tolerated it. Aldo kept me sane. Our friendship is the strongest one I have. Even more than Luca. Solid in a way I can only share with Aldo. I try to be that for him, but I think he was missing something." He looked at me. "He was missing you. I had Nonna as my soft spot. He needs you, doll."

"Why do you call me that?"

He shrugged. "I dunno. I like it. I don't mean it in a disrespectful way."

"I don't feel it that way either. You just don't seem the nickname sort of guy."

He laughed in agreement. "I'm not."

"What about your future, Roman? Will there be another soft spot? Will the warrior take a bride?"

He shook his head. "No. I have no interest in a bride or a family. Luca, yes. I see Aldo with you and a family. Me? No. I think my father killed that in me. He took something from each of us. That was what he stole from me. He took Luca's youth and innocence and twisted it. Mine too, I suppose, but even worse, he stole my future—my ability to love."

"That is so sad. And wrong."

"It is what it is."

"No. I mean you're wrong. I think you can love. I just think you need to find the right person to show that love to."

He flashed me a grin, but I saw the pain in his eyes. "I doubt it, doll, but thanks for the vote of confidence." He stood. "Now, how about some dinner, and I'll tell you all about Aldo as a kid."

I knew the subject was closed.

"Sure."

Aldo

I watched Vi, fascinated at her display of bravery. She insisted on going back to the deli. A week of "doing nothing" was enough for her. She donned a new uniform, one with longer sleeves, tied a pretty scarf around her neck, and walked into the restaurant as if it was just another day. Wanda greeted her with open arms, and I felt the wave of pride wash over me as I studied her. I knew Violet was nervous and hiding it. But I was the only one. To everyone else, she was simply Vi. They all thought she'd had the flu—she wanted no one to know about the attack. Wanda suspected something but kept it to herself. That was one reason she'd been such a longtime employee. She kept her thoughts and ideas to herself.

Roman came up behind me, folding his arms over his chest. "How is she?"

"Brilliant."

He huffed a breath. "Hardly surprising."

I had to laugh. He was very fond of her, which surprised me since Roman didn't tend to like many people. But he found her funny and smart. The fact that he visited her during her recovery told me how much he liked her. Roman rarely left the casino unless it was for his nonna or brother. I liked the fact that he approved.

"Everything ready for the wedding?"

"Yes. Judith has it all in hand. Luca and Justine want it over so they can move on with their life together. Her father is a bit of a stickler, to say the least. Her brother is slowly coming to terms with the fact that he can't control her anymore. He and Luca lock horns almost daily, though. It is rather amusing listening to Luca tell Mason to fuck off."

"Luca wants her to fly," I commented, watching Vi smile and slide a plate in front of a woman. She glanced up and saw me looking at her. She shook her head and walked back toward the kitchen, but she was still smiling. She knew I would check in on her frequently. It was a compulsion for me. The man who attacked her was dead and gone, but we both had scars that were still healing from the ordeal.

"Mason is remarkably old-fashioned when it comes to his sister. I wonder what his wife is like," Roman mused. "I suppose I'll meet her this weekend."

I nodded, not speaking. I cast one last glance toward the restaurant and turned to go into the hotel.

"What about you?" he asked as we walked the lobby, checking on everything before heading to the high-roller room.

"What about me?"

"When are you going to admit you love Vi and put a ring on her finger?"

"Leave it alone, Roman. That is between us."

He shook his head. "Don't lose the best thing in your life because you're scared. That isn't the Aldo I know. He faces his fears head on."

Then he turned and walked away, leaving me staring after him.

CHAPTER 17
ALDO

The day of the wedding, Vi spent at the hotel. I was making sure everything was running all right, freeing up Roman to have time with his brother. Vi spent a few hours at the spa, the massage and beauty treatments helping her healing, to get ready for the evening. The ceremony was at six, pictures happening before and after. The reception began immediately, followed by dancing.

I headed upstairs for a quick shower, then I would change and we would head down to the wedding. Vi was incredibly relaxed, not bothered at all about having to be early or worrying about what she would do while I was busy helping make sure things went off without a hitch. Roman was worried about some of the people attending. Older members of the syndicate who already frowned at Luca's ways of doing things. Now marrying outside the larger circle, unlike the old days, where marriages were usually methods of strengthening ties between the larger, more important families. If their father were alive, that was exactly what would have occurred, but as with many of Mr. Costas's ideas, Luca let them die with their father and created a new path. There was no doubt he was wildly in love with his wife and didn't care who knew it. She was obviously as smitten as he was, and together they made a stunning couple.

I walked into the hotel suite, smiling at Vi, who was sitting in the chair, wrapped in a fluffy robe. Her makeup was done, and she was already breathtaking. I bent to kiss her, pleased at the clever application of makeup on her throat. The bruising was hardly visible, and I knew her dress had a neckline that would further conceal the injuries.

"I need twenty minutes," I said.

She laughed. "So unfair. I take all afternoon, and you'll walk into the bathroom and emerge looking like something out of *GQ* in less than half an hour."

I chuckled. "But you are beyond beautiful, and beside you, I'll look like a schmuck."

She shook her head. "Impossible. You'll be the sexiest man there."

I kissed her again. "That's why I keep you around."

A flash of hurt tore through her expression, but she didn't comment. "Go get ready. I'll put on my dress while you're in the shower."

I was out in ten minutes, freshly shaved. I towel-dried my hair and walked into the room, stopping at the vision in front of me. Vi's dress was a deep, rich blue that set off her creamy skin. It was simple, with a tight bodice and layered fabric that swirled around her ankles. The neckline was intricate with beadwork, and the long, sheer sleeves had matching trim around the wrists. The skirt sparkled in the light of the room. Somehow it was sexier than a revealing dress. It was elegant and refined, and she looked like a million bucks.

She smiled at my low whistle.

"Baby, you are stunning."

"Thank you."

She watched me dress, and I felt her eyes on me like a caress touching every part of my body. "Stop it."

She laughed. "I'm just looking." That remark was followed by a sigh. "It's all you allow these days."

I shrugged on my jacket, pulling at my tie to get it to lie flat. "You've been hurt," I said firmly. I hadn't attempted to make love to her since she was attacked. She was too vulnerable at first, and I couldn't seem to get that image out of my mind. I didn't want to hurt her in any capacity.

She came over, tapping my hands out of the way and fiddling with the tie so it sat correctly. "And as I keep telling you, I am healed."

"Soon."

She glanced down. "Your dick is in agreement with me."

"My dick will get over it."

She looked sad as she picked up her purse. "I hope we all do," she murmured. She shut her eyes, tossing her hair. It had gotten longer, brushing the nape of her neck. I liked to run my fingers through it at night. The action calmed me.

"Ready to go?"

I nodded. "Vi…"

She looked at me. "What?"

"I don't dance."

"What do you mean?"

"I don't dance. I am terrible at it. Even Nonna V agrees with me. So I won't dance with you tonight."

"You won't even try?"

"No."

The sadness in her eyes grew, but she nodded. "That's fine, Aldo. We can attend the wedding and dinner and leave shortly after. You can use my health as an excuse."

I was surprised by her reply. "That would work."

"Well then," she said, smiling brightly, the action so fake, even I knew it. "At least I am good in some capacity. Let's go."

I began to protest, but she opened the door and headed down the hall. I followed her, cursing myself. I should have told her another way. It was obvious she thought I was making up an excuse not to touch her. I looked at her as the elevator came, the door opening. I stepped in beside her, reaching for her hand. She let me take it, but there was no answering grasp from her fingers. Instead, her palm rested in mine, lax and unresponsive.

"Baby," I began.

"No," she replied. "You don't dance. No big deal. Drop it."

"I am really awful. I don't want to risk hurting you."

"That's the theme of the day, isn't it?"

The elevator opened, and another couple stepped on, halting our conversation. When we arrived on our floor and the door opened, Vi spied Nonna V and went over to say hello. Roman caught my eye, and I went to help him. When I looked over my shoulder, Vi was walking away with Nonna V, not even sparing me a glance.

I would have to talk to her later.

VI

The room was breathtaking, lit with hundreds of candles and decorated with flowers and ribbons in a soft peach color. The tables were set with fine linens and china, and the dance floor expansive and gleaming under the huge chandelier over it. The other half of the room was set up with an altar, the chairs in neat rows, waiting for the ceremony.

Aldo had told me it wasn't a large wedding, but a hundred people seemed large to me. He also told me most were from her side and that Luca's were mostly business-related, with a few friends added to the list. Looking around the room, I had a feeling there were a lot of powerful men here. I knew Luca and Justine were already married, but the invited guests didn't know that. It was something only family knew.

And me.

I wasn't family.

I had no idea what was going on with Aldo. He had been tense the past few days. Withdrawn and quiet. And as I pointed out, he hadn't touched me since the incident. Oh, he cared for me, helped me bathe, rubbed medicine onto my skin, and dropped gentle kisses to my head and lips, but nothing else. I turned to Nonna V. "Is it true Aldo doesn't dance?"

She grimaced. "He is terrible. I tried to teach him. He stepped on my toes so often, I had to stop."

"Oh." Somehow hearing her confirm it helped.

"Roman loves to dance. So does Luca. Aldo, not so much. He said something?"

"Yes. He said no dancing."

She chuckled. "Probably for the best. Your feet will thank you."

"Ah."

"Roman will dance with you. He will dance with me and with Justine. Then he will escort me to my room."

"You don't want to stay?"

She looked mischievous. "By the time the men speak, it will be late. The hot air in here will be unbearable."

I covered my mouth as I laughed.

"Roman and Luca will be short. Her side, I think not. Make sure you have a drink close at hand."

I nodded sagely.

A moment later, Roman appeared to escort Nonna V to her seat. He smiled at me. "You look beautiful today, Vi."

"Thank you. You clean up pretty well—for a *gangsta*," I added with a whisper.

He chuckled and led Nonna toward the front of the chairs. Aldo stepped up, crooking his elbow. I took it, smiling at him. He wasn't lying about dancing. The rest, we'd have to address later, but this wasn't the time. He smiled back, looking handsome, and took me close to the back, leaving a chair empty. "For me," he instructed.

"Okay."

He hesitated, then leaned down and kissed me. "Thank you," he breathed out, moving away before I could ask him why.

The man was as much a mystery to me at times now as he'd been the first day I'd met him.

I wondered if it would ever change.

ALDO

I relaxed once the ceremony was over, the speeches done, and the dancing began. No one had stepped out of line, tried to stop the ceremony, or bring up business. Everything was going well. Luca and Justine were happy and married in a way that pleased her father, and they would now be able to experience their lives out in the open with each other. He was obviously crazy for her, and it was good to see. Nonna V beamed during the ceremony and was still smiling, although she looked a little tired. She had danced with Luca, and I knew once she danced with Roman, she would leave.

I glanced at Vi, who was watching the room and seemed to be enjoying herself. She had danced with Luca as well, and I admired how lovely she looked on the floor. Several men had come over to ask her, but she had declined politely, leaning toward me in her chair as she did so. My hand on her shoulder told them she was taken, and they didn't linger long.

I couldn't blame them. She was beautiful tonight in the candlelight. Her dress set off her dark hair and lovely eyes, and when she moved, she was graceful.

Elegant. And completely sexy. My cock had been hard the entire night, wanting her.

Keeping my hands off her had been the hardest thing I'd ever done. But the thought of causing her pain kept my libido in check every day. I tried to show her my affection, but I was beginning to think I had failed.

And I had never expressed out loud the way I felt about her. The thought of living without her had become unfathomable. I'd heard her mention to Wanda she'd be moving back to her place in a few days, and the idea that she wouldn't be there, at the house, with me, threw me into a tailspin.

I had bought the house as a place to put down roots. But once I'd bought it, I rarely stayed. The hotel was easier. Less lonely somehow. But since Vi had been there, the house felt like home. We cooked together on occasion—neither of us great, but it was fun, because it was with her. Knowing she was waiting for me when I got home made me hurry a little faster to get to her. I lingered there long after I should have gone to the casino. I looked forward to the day her injuries were totally healed and she would join me in bed the way she used to before the attack.

Roman approached and offered his hand to Vi. "Dance, doll?"

She stood and took his proffered hand. For some reason, that bothered me. I turned and studied them on the dance floor.

"So elegant," Nonna V said. "They dance well together."

"He's a little short for her," I replied.

"He is the perfect height. Not all can tower over the general population, you know. They move very well."

They did. Both were graceful and fluid. I narrowed my eyes. His hand was a little close to her ass.

That was my ass to touch.

"He is fond of her."

I huffed a snort.

"He calls her doll. I'm not sure Roman has ever given someone a nickname."

He did call her doll. It never bothered me until Nonna V pointed it out. I was sure Vi preferred it when I called her baby. She always smiled when I did.

At least, she used to.

I looked again. The bastard was holding her far too closely.

And she was leaning her head on his shoulder.

What the fuck?

She lifted her head and said something to him, and he nodded. They stopped dancing and headed out to the balcony, disappearing through the door. Together.

I blinked. She didn't come back to the table. To me.

She went with Roman.

Red-hot anger tore through me. Jealousy, a feeling I had never experienced, raged inside my chest, and of their own volition, my hands clenched into fists on the table.

Nonna V looked at me, then toward the balcony doors. "Oh dear," she murmured.

I stood, my feet carrying me across the floor, ignoring everyone around me. I dodged couples and people carrying drinks. My focus was on one place.

I stormed onto the balcony, ready for a fight. Prepared to end a friendship of a lifetime.

Except, Roman was seated at a table, his head bent over the phone in his hand. Vi was by the rail, staring at the view. Roman looked up as I appeared, a slow grin on his face.

"Took you long enough." He stood, clapping me on the shoulder. "Go get your girl."

"What?" I sputtered.

"Me and Nonna. What a team."

Then he strolled away, whistling. Vi glanced over her shoulder. "You didn't really fall for that."

"Of course not."

She turned, leaning back against the rail. "Yet, here you are."

My anger peaked, and I covered the space between us quickly. "No more dancing with the Costas brothers. Or anyone else."

"Is that a fact?" she murmured. "Who will I dance with?"

"Me." I yanked her into my arms. "And I don't want to hear a word about your toes."

Except as I began to move, my body felt different. In sync with hers. Vi sighed and leaned her head on my chest. It fit there far better than it had on Roman's shoulder.

"See?" she whispered. "You can dance. You just needed the right partner." She lifted her hand, running her fingers over my neck. "We always move well together." She nestled closer, clutching my back. "People say dancing is like making love standing up."

I grunted. We made love well. Then it hit me. She was right. I was dancing with her. Slowly, not as gracefully as Roman, but we moved together.

She fit me perfectly.

Everywhere.

She always had.

And she always would.

I stopped, looking down at her. Her eyes glittered in the light. "Tell me," I said. "Tell me your words again."

She swallowed, looking nervous. "I love you, Aldo Ricci."

"I love you, Violet Nelson. Every fucking thing about you. You were made for me."

The glitter became liquid, and tears spilled over her cheeks. "Yes, I was. Took you long enough to figure it out."

"I know and I'm sorry. The feelings were there for a long time, but it took me a while to find the words." I bent and captured her mouth, tasting her tears and her smile. Tasting her love that had always been there.

"You're not going back to your apartment."

"I'm not?"

"No. You're staying with me at the house. Because when you're there, it's a home, and I want to share that home with you. You've been looking for a place to belong. You found it. With me."

"You've been saving up lots of words, I see. Anything else?"

"We're getting married."

"Right now?"

"Soon. You want that?" I indicated the room.

"God, no. Something small."

"I'll arrange it. Wear something that shows off your legs. I fucking love your legs."

"Anything more to add?"

"No more working. My wife doesn't need to work."

"Is that so?"

"Yes. No point anyway. I'm going to get you pregnant, and we're gonna fill that house with babies."

"You're awfully bossy for someone who hasn't fucked me in weeks and just learned to use their words."

I stopped moving, staring down at her. "It's been eleven days, six hours, and forty-seven minutes since I was last inside you. That is going to change in the next fifteen minutes. We're going inside, saying good night, and if you take too long, some people in there are going to get a show they didn't bargain for and Luca will never speak to me again."

"And then?" she whispered breathlessly.

"I am taking you upstairs, and I'm going to fuck you until you pass out. I won't hurt you, but you will know exactly who you belong to. Then tomorrow, we're going to the jewelry store, and I'm getting you the biggest fucking rock I can find. No one will doubt you're taken."

"You sound pretty sure of yourself."

I wrapped my hand around the back of her neck, pulling her close. "I am because I love you and you love me. We were meant to be together. I'm the shadow, and you're the light. We need each other."

Her smile was brilliant. "Well, why didn't you just say that?"

I began to laugh.

"I love you, baby. I'll spend the rest of my life showing you just how much. If you let me."

"Love you right back, big man. Now go back to being bossy and take me to your room."

I kissed her.

"Let's go."

CHAPTER 18
VI

We made it out of the reception without speaking to anyone. The bride and groom were dancing, locked in their own world. Roman was with Nonna V, and he winked at us as we went past. Aldo flipped him off subtly, which made me grin and Roman's smile get wider.

In the elevator, Aldo kept me tucked to his side. He looked calm and aloof, but I saw the storm behind his eyes, and I prepared myself for when he released its fury.

I could hardly wait.

In the suite, I turned to him, our gazes locked. For the first time, I saw everything he kept hidden away. The love and devotion in his stare were blatant. Rich, filled with promise, the future laid out plainly.

I was his future.

He cupped my face and kissed me the way he always did. Sweetly, passionately at first, until the fire overcame him and it turned carnal. Deep. Wet. Passionate.

But he didn't rush. He didn't tear off my dress, throw me on the bed, and fuck me. Instead, he turned me around, undoing my dress and letting it pool to the floor in a swath of rich blue. Then slowly, carefully, he kissed every scar, mark, and place where a bruise had been inflicted. His mouth was gentle, worshipping.

He whispered soft words of adoration. Affection. Affirmation.

Love.

With every touch, he healed me. Reclaimed me in a way that left no doubt of his feelings. I felt his love settle into my heart, my soul, my very being.

And for the first time, I belonged.

To him.

He lifted my chin, smiling. "And I belong to you."

"Make me yours again, Aldo."

Moments later, we were skin to skin, our clothes left behind on the floor, discarded quickly. His body covered mine, the heat and weight of him welcome. Needed. We kissed endlessly. Touched everywhere. Reacquainted ourselves with each other until we were breathless and aching with desire. He hovered over me as he slid inside, and I wrapped my legs around him, groaning at the feeling of rightness. He stilled, shutting his eyes. "This," he murmured. "Always this."

He began to move, our eyes holding, the passion between us quickly becoming an inferno. The slide and feel of him inside me was overwhelming. The heat of our bodies pressed together, a fire that raged. My orgasm caught me off guard, fast and intense. He rode it out, never faltering as I quaked and cried out his name. He sat back, pulling me upright, surrounding me with his body, his embrace tight. He buried his face into my neck, driving into me harder and faster, catching me back up in another wave of pleasure so intense, I whimpered.

"Give me another one," he demanded, his movements sharp and powerful.

I fell again, and he came with me, our orgasms long, loud, and so satisfying.

Then we dropped back to the bed, sated, exhausted, and happy.

For now.

He kissed my brow. "I'm taking you home, and we're doing that all over again, baby. In our bed."

I snuggled closer. "Okay. Nap first."

He laughed softly. "Nap first."

ALDO

Vi fell asleep, and I stared down at her in wonder. I had missed her silken skin and the taste of her, musky and rich on my tongue. I loved how she felt under my hands. The way she blossomed and moved with me. Her scent was intoxicating, and I inhaled it, greedy and wanting.

How I could have denied the love I felt for her was a mystery. It was all so clear now. She was my everything. The one thing I refused to give up. I understood the sudden change in Luca now. Violet Nelson had become the epicenter of my world, and now it would revolve around her.

Always.

I had been an idiot. No doubt I would be again. I pressed a gentle kiss to her head, knowing she would somehow forgive me next time.

She stirred, and I pulled her tighter to my chest. "Time to go?" she mumbled.

"Soon, baby."

"M'kay."

She was out again, and with a sigh, I shut my eyes, relaxing into sleep. We were both going to need it for what I had planned.

It was late when we woke up the next day. I had woken up around two, and we had dressed and come back to the house, Vi laughing as I swooped her into my arms and carried her over the threshold.

"We're not married yet," she admonished me.

"Don't care. We're walking in as official. I get to carry you."

"I never thought someone could with how tall I am."

"I'll carry you anywhere."

Then I took her upstairs to our room and fucked her. Once on the bed, then in the shower, and finally, lazy and slow under the blankets, as dawn broke through the night, filling the room with its diffused splendor.

Then we slept, wrapped around each other.

I slipped from the warm bed, pulling on the sweats I'd worn home from the hotel. I left Vi sleeping and went downstairs, making coffee and putting a pan of frozen cinnamon rolls in the oven before heading to the den and taking something from the safe. I slid the dusty box into my pocket and headed back to the kitchen, knowing the scent of coffee would wake her soon.

She appeared as I finished a few emails and texts, including one from Roman telling me to take the day off and he would cover. I knew the next while would be challenging for him with Luca gone, so I appreciated the time.

I looked up as she walked in, wearing my shirt, her hair mussed, sleep lines on her face from her pillow and traces of my scruff and bite marks on her skin.

She was gorgeous.

I pulled her close and kissed her, chuckling as she looked toward the counter, anticipation in her eyes.

"Done with me, baby? Coffee more important?"

"I need it if you plan on more ravishing."

"Get a big cup, then. I have the day off."

She waggled her eyebrows. "Excellent."

I pulled the cinnamon buns from the oven and chuckled as she ate two in a row, barely chewing.

"Hungry?" I asked.

"You depleted me."

I threw back my head in laughter, watching as she licked her fingers clean. "I was feeling fairly depleted myself, but seeing you in my shirt and licking those pretty fingers, I'm suddenly awake again."

She rolled her eyes. "Typical male."

"Get used to it."

A shadow crossed her face. "Did you mean it, Aldo?"

"Mean what?"

"Last night. That you loved me. And wanted to, ah…" She trailed off, looking uncertain.

"Marry you?" I finished. "Knock you up?" I leaned forward, pulling her hand from worrying the hem of my shirt. "Every word."

She smiled. "Good."

I slid the box her way. "The jewelry stores are closed. Maybe you can wear this until we get there, so every time you look down, you remember I meant it."

She hesitated, then drew the box toward her. She opened the lid and stared at the contents. "It was my mother's," I explained. "My father gave it to her, and she always wore it with her band. He could never afford a big diamond, but she loved this ring. I'd like you to have it. To wear it."

She pulled the ring out, looking at it in the light. The circlet of pearls was old, but the pearls' luster was obvious even now. The gold was still thick, and tiny diamonds dotted the band.

"It's lovely."

I plucked it from her fingers and slid it on her left hand. It fit her and looked pretty. I bent and kissed her hand. "Until we choose your forever ring."

"This is my forever ring. You put it on my hand."

I smiled at her sentimental thought. "I'd like to give you a diamond."

She laughed. "I would love that too, but I will always love this ring because you gave it to me and it means so much to you."

I bent forward and she met me partway, and we kissed.

I sat back. "I'll apply for the license this week. Roman is going to be crazy while Luca is gone. Would you mind waiting to get married until they're back? I don't want to leave him alone without Luca or me around."

"I don't mind at all. We don't have to rush."

I shook my head in amusement. "Listen to you, the voice of reason. I suddenly understand Luca's need to fly Justine to Vegas. I want to marry you now. Today. I want our life to start now."

"It has, Aldo. I'm not going anywhere. You can get all my stuff from the apartment. I'll move in."

"That's great, but it isn't enough. I want the world to know you're mine." I rolled my shoulders, unable to explain the need I was feeling.

She cupped my face. "Hey, I get it. But be patient. Roman is dealing with enough without you getting married the day after his brother. He needs you right now, and I'm right here."

I huffed a sigh. "Fine. I'll try. How big a wedding do you want?"

"Very small."

"Here?"

She pursed her lips. "Is there a place in the hotel we could do it that isn't massive? I'm talking a dozen people."

"There is a suite on the top floor. All windows overlooking the Falls. It's breathtaking. Used for a lot of small weddings. We could get married there. Do a lunch or dinner." I frowned. "You don't want the dancing and speeches and all that? The big dress and the music?"

She shook her head. "Oh, I want the dress. Something spectacular. But a few people, some champagne, and flowers. Pictures." She paused. "A honeymoon?"

I laughed. "Roman will gift us a honeymoon—that's his thing. Wherever we want to go."

"Somewhere warm, with a beach where I can be alone with you."

I grinned. "Done."

I pulled up a calendar on my phone and showed it to her. "How about there?" I pointed to a date six weeks away. "You can get your dress, I'll help Roman, and then we'll get married." I double-checked the internal database. "The room I'm thinking about is free on the Thursday. Or I can ask Judith to kick out the people—"

She shook her head, interrupting me. "I don't care the day of the week we get married, as long as I get to marry you."

"I'll get Maurice to block it and let Judith know."

She beamed at me. "Perfect."

I pulled her to my lap and kissed her. "Yeah, baby. Perfect."

EPILOGUE - ALDO

Sun bounced off the Falls, the light reflecting and scattering across the room. I rolled my shoulders, tense and ready to jump out of my skin. Roman chuckled beside me. "She's behind the doorway, Aldo. You'll see her in a minute."

A minute was too long. I had waited patiently for Luca to return from his honeymoon. For Roman to hand back the reins. For this day, this *minute* to arrive. I didn't want to wait another sixty seconds.

I wanted Violet beside me so we could say our vows and be married.

The door opened, and Vi stepped into the room, robbing me of all my breath. She was stunning.

Her dress was ivory, molded to her body, leaving her shoulders and upper arms bare, the lace glittering with crystals. Sleeves started partway down her arms, circled tightly at her wrists. The dress hugged her waist and ended mid-thigh, showing off her sexy legs. A pouf of lace and tulle exploded from her hips into a long train that trailed behind her. I had to shut my eyes for a moment and lock down my body, wondering if asking her to show off her legs had been a good idea. My cock was doing its damned best to embarrass me, and I had a feeling an erection at the altar wasn't the best look.

Roman clapped me on the shoulder. "You are one lucky bastard."

Luckily, his voice cleared the lust, and I lifted my eyes back to my bride as she walked toward me. Her smile and the mischievous twinkle in her eye made me aware she knew exactly what I was thinking.

It was a small group around us. Roman, Nonna V, Luca, and Justine. Wanda and a couple of friends from the deli. A few close business acquaintances. Only twelve people—exactly what Vi wanted. I made sure there were flowers, lots of champagne, and I wore a tuxedo.

And cake. She'd asked for lots of cake. As far as I was concerned, if she agreed to marry me, she got anything she wanted.

But she was taking too damn long to reach me. When had the room become so big?

I stepped forward, reaching out my hand, and she smiled as she extended hers to clasp mine, letting me pull her closer.

The justice of the peace smiled and performed the brief ceremony. I slid my mother's ring back into place on her finger, knowing Vi would add the diamond that I had bought her back with it. The large, four-carat cushion cut ring was on her right hand at the moment. The fact that she loved the small pearl ring more than the big diamond made me adore this woman more than I thought possible.

She slipped a thick gold band onto my finger, and I made a fist, liking how the weight felt on my hand. We were pronounced husband and wife, and I smiled. "Finally."

I took great joy in kissing my wife.

My wife.

Such a small word for a person who changed my life and made me a better man. Who filled my world with joy and laughter and could brighten my day with a simple smile.

She was my world.

My everything.

And I would spend the rest of my life showing her.

VI

The sun was high in the sky, a ball of fire in the bright blue. I stretched out on my blanket, sitting up and shading my eyes, looking for Aldo. Sun glinted off the ridiculously huge diamond on my hand, casting rays on the sand. It was crazy and unnecessary, and I loved it.

Aldo came into view, and I tried not to laugh. This was his third time out jogging today. He'd gone four times yesterday. Plus, fucked me in the ocean, the hammock, on the bed, and once on the deck.

My husband was going stir-crazy.

The first few days were blissful. We stayed up late, making love, talking, walking the private beach. We went sailing, snorkeling, and napped in the sun. He tried parasailing and made love to me on every surface of the small beach house. We ate meals cooked by a private chef. There was a butler who brought fresh drinks and snacks to the beach house any time we called. Otherwise, we were alone. It was glorious. I read on the beach and by the pool, never knowing such decadence. There was nowhere to go. Nothing else to do. For the first time in my adult life, I had no job, no responsibilities.

By day six, I noticed Aldo was getting a bit restless. His jogs were longer. I caught him checking his emails while lying in the hammock, quickly putting his phone away if he saw me looking. He found an excuse to head to the main resort area and was gone for a while, making up the excuse of watching something on the screen in the lounge. I had no doubt he was answering emails and making calls.

Yesterday, he prowled the beach, jogged, swam. Made love to me until I was exhausted. But he didn't say a word about being bored. The fact was that the man had no idea how to relax, but he didn't want to ruin our honeymoon.

I watched as he headed directly into the ocean, diving under and swimming in the clear blue waves. I got up and joined him, floating around in the beautiful water. He swam close, pulling me to him and kissing me. I could taste the salt of the water on his lips and feel the heat of the sun on his skin.

"Good run?" I asked innocently.

"Yeah, it was great."

"They have movie night at the main beach tonight if you want to go," I offered. "Something different."

He shrugged. "I'm happy here with you."

"Anything special you'd like to do tomorrow? More parasailing? Go out on the boat?"

"Maybe the boat."

"One last trip would be nice," I said.

He frowned. "We can go as much as you want."

I hooked my arms around his neck. "If there was something I wanted, could I have it?"

"Anything."

"I changed our flights. We're leaving tomorrow night."

He gaped at me. "What?"

I laughed. "Aldo, you're going stir-crazy here. If you keep jogging and fucking me to pass the time, one of us is going to end up dead from exhaustion."

"No—we're on our honeymoon! We can't go back early."

"Yes, we can. We can take another trip in a few months. A five-day one. I think that's as long as you can handle." I shook my head. "You aren't so good with the whole relaxing thing."

He looked crestfallen. "I'm sorry."

I cupped his face. "I'm not. I've had a wonderful time, and I would love to come back. But we need shorter vacations until you can learn to unwind and separate."

"I'll try harder."

"If you have to try to relax, then you're missing the point. I'm not upset. As long as we go home together, that is all that matters." I nestled my head onto his shoulder. "You can keep trying to get me pregnant there."

He tightened his arms. "We do have a comfortable bed at home."

"We do."

"I could make you coffee in the morning."

"You could."

He looked down at me, clearly worried. "You wouldn't be unhappy?"

"Promise me you'll bring me back here for another week. Promise me we'll do other short trips."

"I promise."

"Promise me you'll tell me what you're feeling so I can share it. Help you."

His gaze softened. "I didn't want to disappoint you."

"You could never."

"I don't know how Luca did it for a month," he confessed.

I laughed. "They traveled a lot, Justine told me. And he was in touch with Roman at times. You've been very good."

"I answered some emails yesterday."

"I know." I drew in a breath. "You ready to go home and start our life?"

"Roman is going to laugh his ass off over this."

"He'll be thrilled you're back. I bet his life has been boring as hell with us gone."

"You're probably right."

"Take me home, Aldo."

He crashed his mouth to mine.

"Absolutely."

OUTTAKE - VI

Aldo walked in, Roman with him. I smiled at them, kissing Aldo on the cheek. “Hungry, boys?”

Aldo nodded. “Starving. It’s been a busy night.”

“I’ll get you the usual. Roman?”

“Clubhouse and salad.”

I chuckled. He ate far better than Aldo. Once we were married, I planned on getting more vegetables into him. Fewer fries.

They headed to a table in the staff section, and I put in the order, adding coffee for Roman and a shake for Aldo. I didn’t have to ask.

Wanda came over with a smile. “I can’t believe I’m losing my best employee. Your last shift is tomorrow.”

She sniffed dramatically. "But I will admit, I have never seen Mr. Ricci smile so much."

I laughed. "Derek is thrilled with the extra hours. And the new girl seems great. She learned the menu and is already rocking it."

Wanda nodded. "I know. But I will miss you."

I waved my hand, the light catching on the huge diamond residing on my finger. I felt odd wearing it to work, but Aldo hated it if I took it off. "I'll be around. I'll come see you when I visit Aldo."

She smiled. "You do that."

I checked on my customers and headed to the kitchen to get the orders for Aldo and Roman. I had to admit, I was excited about no longer working. I had no idea what the future had in store, but the thought of not being on my feet for eight hours a day was a good one. Once we were married and back from our honeymoon, I would figure out my path.

I took the plates and gave them to my two favorite men, refilling Roman's coffee and getting my sandwich, sitting beside Aldo. He squeezed my leg, and we talked about nothing and everything.

"You still sure you want to marry this guy, doll? I can get you a bus ticket outta town," Roman teased.

I chuckled. "A bus ticket. Tempting, but I'll stick with him."

He grinned, swallowing a mouthful of his club sandwich. "Only the best."

I finished my sandwich and swiped the last fries off Aldo's plate. "Thanks for the offer."

"Ends tomorrow. No turning back." His eyes twinkled in glee. Aldo glared at him, and I laughed, elbowing him playfully.

"Stop reacting to it. That's why he does it."

I stood and took the plates to the kitchen, reaching for the coffeepot. A couple walked into the deli, and I froze as I stared at them, unable to move. They didn't notice me, and the new girl went over and handed them menus. I stepped back behind the wall so they didn't see me.

Aldo appeared by my elbow. "Vi, baby, what is it?"

I looked at him, and Roman stood, coming over. "What's going on?"

I blinked at them.

"Barry—the guy who stole my money and all my stuff…and my friend, well, my ex-friend, Marie, they just walked in."

Roman looked around the corner then back at me. "The guy with the slicked-back hair?"

I nodded.

"He looks like a douche."

"He didn't wear his hair like that before."

He shrugged. "You've traded up, that's for sure."

Aldo looked at Roman. "I think the night just got a little better."

Roman grinned, covertly snapping a picture of Barry. "We could have fun with this."

"Lots of fun."

"How much did he steal?"

"Um, about fifteen hundred plus whatever he got for selling all my stuff." I frowned, shaking my head. "Leave it. It doesn't matter anymore."

Aldo pressed a kiss to my head. "That, baby, is where you are wrong. It matters to me."

I didn't like the look in his eyes. "If he hadn't done that, I wouldn't have met you."

He nodded. "You're right."

"We won't kill him, then," Roman mused. "But we can teach him a lesson."

"Stop it," I hissed.

Roman looked at his phone. "Well, look here. Mr. Barry is currently having a good night at the machines. He's turned twenty bucks into two thousand. He hasn't cashed out yet, though."

"Hmm. Shame if his luck turned."

"A real shame."

Aldo kissed me. "See you later, baby. Stay back here for now. You're done for the night."

There was no point arguing. I knew that look. On both their faces.

I kissed him, and he caught my face in his hands. "Go up to the room and relax. I'll come get you."

I wagged my finger at both of them. "No blood."

Roman grinned. Widely. "Can't promise that. Sorry, doll."

He paused. "What does he drink?"

I shuddered. "Tequila. Loves the stuff."

I watched them go, shaking my head.

What were they going to do?

Aldo

Roman turned on the charm, introducing himself to a few tables, loud enough that asswipe could hear him. Roman winked at me as we approached the table where our target sat.

We stopped, Roman offering a smile. "Enjoying your night?"

They looked up, Barry instantly becoming an ass-kisser. "Oh yeah, man. Having a great time. Fabulous casino. One of the best I've seen." He leaned back, almost preening. "I've taken a lot of your money tonight."

I wanted to laugh. Two grand was a cup of coffee to Roman. And I would bet a million bucks Barry had never been to a better casino. He was going to regret walking into this one.

Roman waved his hand. "That's how it rolls. You doing slots? Blackjack? Cards?"

"Slots. I'd like to do cards. I'm great at poker."

Roman looked suitably impressed. "There's a game happening in about thirty minutes. Buy-in is a grand."

Marie leaned over the table. "We should just eat and go."

Barry ignored her. "I'm on a hot streak tonight. A grand isn't a problem."

Marie grabbed his arm. "Barry—"

He shook her off. “Shut up,” he said quietly. “I’m doing business here.”

“The money,” she hissed.

“I’ll make us a lot more.”

Roman pulled out his card and handed it to Barry. “Third floor. Private game. You’ll be brought to the room.” He glanced at Marie. “Alone.”

“Understood.”

“Thirty minutes. Oh, and dinner is on the house.”

I followed him out.

“Get the guys together.”

“Which dealer?”

“Samantha. She’s the best, and she’ll distract him.”

We stepped into the elevator. “You about to take him on the ride of his life?”

Roman grinned. “A fucking roller coaster.”

Three hours later, I was doing everything I could not to laugh. Barry had no idea which way was up. He’d been up, down, almost broke, up to twenty grand, and now back down to ten grand. He stared at the chips in front of him and his cards. He had three of a kind, and he was banking on the match. Trying to decide whether he should bluff.

A smarter man would have walked away, but Barry wasn't smart. He was convinced he could rise yet again.

The man across from him had a royal flush. Or would once the final cards were dealt. Al was sweating profusely, tapping at his cards, muttering, his act perfection. He'd hardly been noticed by Barry until now, and I knew Barry was certain he had him beat. He proved it in the next moment, pushing his chips into the center.

"All in."

He met my eyes, smirking in satisfaction. His were slightly blurry. He'd had a few too many free shots of tequila. Roman made sure the good stuff was out.

Everyone had folded but the two of them. His opponent sighed, appeared to be about to fold, then nodded, and pushed his chips in. "Done."

The last card was dealt, and Barry's face almost broke in two with his smile. He laid down his cards. "Four of a kind." He began to stand. "Thanks for this—"

He reached for the pot, but Al stopped him. "Not so fast, kid." He tossed his cards on the table.

"Royal flush."

Barry sat down, his mouth gaping open like a fish. "But—"

Roman stepped forward. "Royal flush beats four of a kind, Barry. You want back in?"

"I'm out of money."

"You owe the house a grand already, but I can give you another loan." Roman smiled, the action not friendly. "Remember the interest, though. It compounds daily."

"Or he compounds your leg," someone laughed.

Barry paled. "No, I guess not." He stared at the table. "I was sure—I mean, I kept turning it around."

Roman shook his head. "Luck always runs out. You need to know how to play the game. And here's a hint. When you're on a hot streak, you don't walk away for a burger." He crossed his arms. "Now, about the grand you owe me."

Barry looked at him, fear in his eyes. "I have no money to pay you. What are you going to do to me?"

Roman leaned on the table, his voice low and scary. "I'm going to give you the biggest break of your life. Get out. Now. Leave. Do not come back to this casino or any property that I own. Because I'll remember you, and it won't just be some bones I break. I will take everything you have. As long as you stay away, the debt is settled. You show back up, it's live again—with interest. And that adds up faster than you can track."

Barry stood, almost falling on his ass to get away from Roman. "Right. Got it. Out of here." He stumbled from the room, mumbling about Marie and how to tell her. I watched him, and after the door closed, Roman thanked everyone, handed them some cash, and offered me a stack. "Three grand for what he took from your girl."

I shook my head. "She won't want it."

"Then donate it in her name."

I took the money and slid it into my pocket.

"Go get Vi and go home," Roman said with a wink. "That was fun watching him fuck himself."

"I bet Marie tells him to do exactly that."

"Revenge is a bitch."

I texted Vi and told her to meet me in the lobby. She replied she was still in the deli, which didn't surprise me. I tugged off my tie and headed downstairs, meeting her just outside the door.

I kissed her hello, cupping her face and enjoying her lips on mine.

"Well?"

"He lost his winnings."

She shook her head, but before she could respond, I heard a low gasp and I turned to see Barry and Marie staring at Vi and me.

Barry looked panicked. Marie shocked. "Violet?" she said.

I wrapped my arm around my fiancée, drawing her close.

"Marie," she said coolly.

"What are you doing here?" Marie asked.

"Waiting for my fiancé."

Marie looked at me, and Barry frowned. "You're the guy who was upstairs. Beside the head guy all night. His bodyguard." He looked between Vi and me. "You're engaged?"

Vi lifted her hand, the light catching the diamond. "Yes."

"Oh man." He stepped forward. "Look, I'm an old friend of Violet's. Couldn't you put in a good word with your boss and get me back in the game? I can turn it around. Pay him back and make back my money. I know I can. I just—"

He was clueless. Really clueless. He had no clue he'd been set up and was thinking only of the big payout that he chased.

I cut him off, pulling his collar tight in my hand. "Listen to me, you little shit. You are no friend of my fiancée. I know who you are, and I know what you did. Be grateful you are walking out of here of your own volition. I'd rather it be a body bag. Got me? If I see your face again, money or no money, what Roman plans on doing to you will seem like a game of slap and tickle. Get the fuck off this property. Now."

His eyes widened, and I smelled the urine that soaked his pants. I stepped back with a disgusted shake of my head and looked at Marie. "You're no better, but I don't hit women. Get out."

For a moment, I was sure he was going to ask again. Marie turned and walked away, heading for the front doors in a hurry.

He was a stupid idiot. I shook my head in warning. "Ten," I said. "Nine…"

He turned and ran.

I looked at Vi, who was watching me. "Slap and tickle?" she said, lifting one eyebrow.

"It fit."

"Did it feel good, scaring him?"

"Not as good as hitting him would have." I showed her the money. "You want this?"

"No."

"We can send it to the homeless shelter."

"Please."

"I doubt we'll see him around again."

She slipped her arm into mine, and we headed for the car. "I agree. He'll never come back." She glanced at me. "Was he a good card player?"

"No. We let him think so. He was up a good amount, but Roman knew exactly how to get him to keep playing. His ego." I chuckled. "That, and the tequila."

She sighed. "I should feel guilty."

I stopped walking. "Why?"

"He lost a lot of money."

I snorted. "His ego took a hit. He lost twenty bucks, baby. Less than what his dinner would have cost him at the deli. You don't have the money until you cash it in. He would have lost it at the machines, because he's one of those people who can't stop. Greedy. So stop feeling guilty. He robbed you and took everything."

"He took *stuff.* I'm the one who ended up with everything. I ended up with you."

I shut my eyes. Jesus, she was going to kill me.

I yanked her close and kissed her. "I love you. You each got what you deserved. Now, forget about him.

Both of them. Forever. They don't deserve your pity or your worry."

"Fine."

I took her hand. "I'm taking you home and making love to you until the sun comes up."

"I can handle that."

I grinned. "Good. I might have a few friends help out."

She began to laugh.

"Bring it on, big man."

I fully intended to.

Thank you so much for reading **ALDO**. If you are so inclined, reviews are always welcome by me at your retailer.

The truth of this book, **ALDO**, is it was never intended to exist. **ROMAN** was written to be a standalone. My beta readers wanted additional backstory for Roman, and I didn't feel a prologue would be long enough. Plus the fact they loved Aldo and Vi's scenes, they wanted their story. What set out to be a short 10k novel turned into this short novel to whet your appetite for Roman's story.

What about Luca and Justine? Keep reading…

Enjoy meeting other readers? Lots of fun, with upcoming book talk and giveaways! Check out Melanie Moreland's Minions on Facebook.

Join my newsletter for up-to-date news, sales, book announcements and excerpts (no spam). Click here to sign up Melanie Moreland's newsletter
or visit my website www.melaniemoreland.com to join.

Scan this QR code and download the behind the pages outtake of the story within the story.

Outtake - The Courtship of Luca and Justine

Enjoy reading! Melanie

ACKNOWLEDGMENTS

As usual, a few thanks.

Lisa, your dedication to your craft always amazes me. So does the number of mistakes you find. That is baffling.

Beth, thank you for your support and insights. You always make my words better. Thank you for asking for this one.

Melissa, Trina, and Deb, thank you for your encouragement, laughter, and support.

Sisters Get Lit.erary Services, thank you for your eagle eyes and assistance. So appreciated!

Karen—as always your support and belief blow me away. I couldn't do this without you. I don't want to even try. You are my friend, my right hand, and my staunchest supporter. I am lucky to have you on my team and in my life.

Atlee and girl George—for all the things you do behind the scenes to help Karen and me—I appreciate every little one. Even when I'm fighting you.

My hype team—you rock. And the way you react to Karen's call to arms is nothing short of inspiring. Thank you.

To all the bloggers, readers, and my promo team. Thank you for everything you do. Shouting your love of books—of my work, posting, sharing—your recommendations keep my TBR list full, and the support you have shown me is deeply appreciated.

My reader group, Melanie's Minions—love you all.

MLM—for all you do I cannot say thank you enough. I wish I could hug you all. Maybe one day.

And my Matthew. Thank you for loving me the way you do. You are in every hero I write.

Always.

ABOUT THE AUTHOR

NYT/WSJ/USAT international bestselling author Melanie Moreland, lives a happy and content life in a quiet area of Ontario with her beloved husband of thirty-plus years and their rescue cat, Amber. Nothing means more to her than her friends and family, and she cherishes every moment spent with them.

While seriously addicted to coffee, and highly challenged with all things computer-related and technical, she relishes baking, cooking, and trying new recipes for people to sample. She loves to throw dinner parties, and enjoys traveling, here and abroad, but finds coming home is always the best part of any trip.

Melanie loves stories, especially paired with a good wine, and enjoys skydiving (free falling over a fleck of dust) extreme snowboarding (falling down stairs) and piloting her own helicopter (tripping over her own feet.) She's learned happily ever afters, even bumpy ones, are all in how you tell the story.

Melanie is represented by Flavia Viotti at Bookcase Literary Agency. For any questions regarding subsidiary or translation rights please contact her at flavia@bookcaseagency.com

- facebook.com/authormoreland
- x.com/morelandmelanie
- instagram.com/morelandmelanie
- bookbub.com/authors/melanie-moreland
- amazon.com/Melanie-Moreland/author/B00GV6LB00
- goodreads.com/Melanie_Moreland
- tiktok.com/@melaniemoreland
- threads.net/@morelandmelanie

ALSO AVAILABLE FROM MORELAND BOOKS

Titles published under M. Moreland

Insta-Spark Collection

It Started with a Kiss

Christmas Sugar

An Instant Connection

An Unexpected Gift

Harvest of Love

An Unexpected Chance

Following Maggie

The Wish List

Titles published under Melanie Moreland

The Contract Series

The Contract (Contract #1)

The Baby Clause (Contract Novella)

The Amendment (Contract #3)

The Addendum (Contract #4)

Vested Interest Series

BAM - The Beginning (Prequel)

Bentley (Vested Interest #1)

Aiden (Vested Interest #2)

Maddox (Vested Interest #3)

Reid (Vested Interest #4)

Van (Vested Interest #5)

Halton (Vested Interest #6)

Sandy (Vested Interest #7)

Vested Interest/ABC Crossover

A Merry Vested Wedding

ABC Corp Series

My Saving Grace (Vested Interest: ABC Corp #1)

Finding Ronan's Heart (Vested Interest: ABC Corp #2)

Loved By Liam (Vested Interest: ABC Corp #3)

Age of Ava (Vested Interest: ABC Corp #4)

Sunshine & Sammy (Vested Interest: ABC Corp #5)

Unscripted With Mila (Vested Interest: ABC Corp #6)

Men of Hidden Justice

The Boss

Second-In-Command

The Commander

The Watcher

The Specialist

Men of the Falls

Aldo

Roman

Reynolds Restorations

Revved to the Maxx

Breaking The Speed Limit

Shifting Gears

Under The Radar

Full Throttle

Full 360

Mission Cove

The Summer of Us

Standalones

Into the Storm

Beneath the Scars

Over the Fence

The Image of You

Changing Roles

Happily Ever After Collection

Heart Strings

My Favorite Kidnapper

www.ingramcontent.com/pod-product-compliance
Lightning Source LLC
LaVergne TN
LVHW012042160826
845678LV00014B/2682

* 9 7 8 1 9 9 0 8 0 3 7 3 4 *